Twilight
Ghost

Also by Magdalen Nabb

Josie Smith
Josie Smith at School
Josie Smith at the Seaside
Josie Smith and Eileen
Josie Smith in Hospital
Josie Smith at Christmas
Josie Smith at the Market
Josie Smith in Winter
Josie Smith in Spring
Josie Smith in Summer
Josie Smith in Autumn

The Enchanted Horse

MAGDALEN NABB

Twilight Ghost

Collins

An imprint of HarperCollins*Publishers*

First published in a German translation by
Diogenes Verlag, AG Zurich in 2000

First published in Great Britain by
Collins in 2002

Collins is an imprint of
HarperCollins*Publishers* Ltd,
77-85 Fulham Palace Road,
Hammersmith, London W6 8JB

The HarperCollins website address is
www.**fire**and**water**.com

1 3 5 7 9 8 6 4 2

ISBN 0 00 713397 9

Printed and bound in Great Britain by
Omnia Books Limited, Glasgow

~ CHAPTER ONE ~

CARRIE LEANED BACK, crushing her hat against the brick wall of the schoolyard, and closed her eyes. The afternoon sun warmed her forehead and hair and she knew, even without looking, that the golden light was coming dappled through the yellow leaves of the chestnut trees that lined the avenue. When she was very small, the first smell of autumn always made her feel excited. She used to start counting the days to Christmas right then. Now she was older it was different, and yet she still had that funny feeling of excitement in her stomach without being sure why. It could be just the start of a new term, new teachers, new exercise books, new pens and pencils. She still liked those things even though she didn't like school any more.

A wet green and yellow leaf fell, brushing her cheek as it passed, and she opened her eyes to look round for her friend.

"Here I am. Let's get going or I'll be late." Katy was already wearing her grey and maroon school scarf in spite of the September sunshine. She lived with her grandmother who always said she was delicate because she was thin and pale, and made her dress warmly. They set off together along the street, kicking through the mounds of orange, red and yellow leaves.

At the corner Carrie said, "I'll walk with you to your dancing class."

"What about your flute lesson?" Katy asked. "It's Wednesday."

"I'm not going," Carrie said. "Forgot my flute."

"Again?" Katy looked worried. Carrie was always getting herself in trouble and she didn't seem to care. "What will your mum say?"

"She won't find out," Carrie said. "She's nearly always out at work now when I get home and May doesn't care. She wouldn't tell, anyway, and there's no point in going if I haven't practised. I hate practising. I hate scales and I hate Miss Swallow as well."

Katy hitched up her bag and walked along without saying anything. She and Carrie had been best friends since infant school and she knew it was no use saying anything when she was in her "I hate everything" mood. It was a shame, though, because Carrie was brilliant at music and everyone, including her mother, thought she was going to be a musician when she grew up.

Carrie hated a lot of things. She hated maths and PE, as well as music lessons, and she hated meat and, more than anything else, she hated the house they'd just moved into.

When they reached the entrance to the ballet school and could hear piano music and a teacher's loud voice, Carrie said, "I'll stay a bit and watch."

"I wish you still came to dancing, too," Katy said. They seemed to do fewer and fewer things together, either because they'd left junior school or because Carrie lived a bit further away now. It was a surprise to Katy that Carrie was walking with her today, but then she couldn't know that Carrie had a secret reason for putting off going home as long as possible.

"I was no good at ballet," Carrie said as they went up the steps and pushed open the glass doors. "Not like you. I just liked the pink tights and the ballet shoes. It was such hard work and I hated getting all sweaty and it hurts your legs and feet. I hated it when Miss Read used to shout and prod at my ankles with that horrible stick of hers. She's so strict it's no fun at all."

"She was a prima ballerina once," Katy said, "and I'm glad she took me in her class. With her I'll have a chance of getting a scholarship."

She ran off to get changed and Carrie sat down halfway up the staircase in the corridor, so she could look into the main studio through the high glass partition. She hadn't been here since she gave up coming to lessons and as she watched the first girls go in, giggling and chattering, to dip their shoes in the resin box, she felt a bit lonely and left out. She watched enviously as a blonde girl in a shiny black leotard tied a scrap of pink ribbon round the coiled plait on top of her head. Her name was Emma, Carrie remembered, and she was a good dancer but not as good as Katy. None of them were as good as Katy. When Katy's gran was so short of money that she had to stop sending her to lessons, Miss Read had told her to come just the same, without paying, because she was so talented. There she was now at the barre, not giggling, not chattering, but warming up, her thin body so frail it seemed impossible that she should be able to spin and jump and curve so beautifully, with every muscle controlled and every gesture graceful. Once, after a particularly horrible lesson with Miss Read, Carrie had asked Katy what it felt like to dance so perfectly. She thought it must be great.

"But it never is perfect," Katy answered, "and you're always thinking and straining to try and be better."

"What's the point, then? There's no fun in that."

"No," Katy answered very quietly, "it's not fun. But sometimes, just sometimes, and only for a little while, you forget about straining and trying, forget about counting bars and fixing your eyes in the right direction, you forget about yourself and just dance. Then it's – not fun – fun's just, you know, messing about with your friends and stuff. It's like… flying… flying so high and so far, you feel as if your heart will burst. Have you never felt like that playing music?"

"No," Carrie had snapped at her. "Never, and I never will either, because I think it's stupid, doing all that work so you can feel as if you're flying.

Quicker to take a plane. I'd rather have fun messing about with my friends, thanks. I hate practising the flute, I just hate it!"

Katy had given her a puzzled look and hadn't answered. Now Carrie was looking down at her through the glass partition, feeling hurt and jealous. Katy was so completely absorbed in what she was doing that there might as well be nobody else in the world. She'd certainly forgotten all about Carrie. Her eyes were fixed on Miss Read who stamped her stick in time to the music and shouted, "*Quatre! Quatre! Quatre! Royale!* Will you straighten those knees, all of you!"

Carrie got up stiffly from the hard wooden staircase and left, the music following her and then fading in the sad afternoon street. She shivered. The sun went down so fast in autumn and now she felt cold and lonelier than ever. She dreaded going home, dreaded approaching the house, but if it went dark it would be more frightening than ever. She started walking faster and faster until she was running. At the corner of Millbridge Road she stopped. Where was the sense in running if danger was ahead of you and safety behind? She stood still a moment, getting her breath and trying to calm down. She told herself, as she did every day, that there was no danger, not real danger, that the terror that made her heart thump and her legs shake wasn't real, couldn't be real. There was nobody up on the top floor except in her imagination. There couldn't be. You couldn't even get up there. She'd asked her mother.

"One day, when we've got things straightened up a bit down here I'll look for the key to the attic stairs door. I can't be bothering about that now."

Carrie forced herself to start walking down Millbridge Road. She felt sick and her mouth was dry. The girl would be there, she knew that for certain, there was no point in trying to pretend she wouldn't. Yet, the truth was that it wasn't really the girl she was frightened of. She was even quite sure it was somebody she knew, and knew really well, though she couldn't exactly decide who. What really frightened her was what happened to the house.

All the houses in Millbridge Road were pretty much the same: big black three-storied buildings with dusty gardens all around them and stone gateposts with huge stone balls on top and the name of the house engraved on the front.

STONELEIGH

The last house on the right and Carrie was standing opposite there now, her fists and stomach squeezed so tight she could hardly breathe for fear of what was about to happen. The door, with a coloured glass fanlight above it, was heavy and panelled and painted dark red. The window frames were painted cream but the paint was old and dirty and peeling. Carrie opened her eyes and tried to keep them fixed on the bay window of the sitting room on the ground floor, her gran's room. She didn't want to look up at the attic, she would not look up at the attic. But somehow she just couldn't help herself. Her gaze was being dragged upwards, against her will, past her parents' bedroom window to the smaller barred one above.

Oh, no! Her legs shook with fear as, just for a moment, she saw the red light of the sunset reflected in the glass behind the bars. Then, just as it always did, the world went dark. The light faded from the sky in seconds and in the gloom, the red reflections vanished. The window was blind and empty. The girl appeared, dressed in white, holding the bars and shaking them. Her mouth was open wide as if she were screaming, but no sound came out.

"I can't help you," Carrie tried to say. "I don't know what to do." But no sound came from her mouth either. She couldn't speak because she couldn't breathe and because the dark world weighed her down with its sadness. But the girl was still there, looking down at her for a long time.

"Who are you? I know you. I'm sure I know you…"

The window went black.

~CHAPTER TWO~

"DO YOU HAVE to lean on the doorbell for ten minutes like there was a fire? Dear God, will you look at the girl! Is it a ghost you've seen, to be turning as white as a sheet?"

"Oh May!" Carrie pushed in at the front door and dropped her bag to hug May for being there, so plump and cheerful and real.

"And what have I done to deserve this?"

"Nothing. Everything. Oh May, I'm glad you're here! I was afraid you might have met your boyfriend and I hate it when you're late – I'll never tell, though, I promise. Oh, I am glad you're here!"

"Is that right? Well, if you want to know, I'd sooner be back in the kitchen. My tea's getting stewed. Do you want a cup? Your little brother's down there, crying into a mug of cocoa."

"He's always crying."

"Missing his mammy," May said, "and his father away, too… poor little eejit. Come and cheer him up and I'll give you both a couple of chocolate biscuits. I've never seen either of you so upset that a nice hot drink and a chocolate biscuit wouldn't set you right."

They went downstairs to the big basement kitchen where James was sniffing, though not crying now, at the table. His face was so streaked with dirty tears you could hardly see his freckles.

"Where have you been?" he shouted at Carrie.

"Flute lesson," Carrie lied.

"You have not!" James was only seven but, somehow, he managed to spy on everything Carrie did and, though he wasn't a tell-tale, he sometimes let things out in front of their parents by accident. How could he possibly know that Carrie had skipped her flute lesson?

"You got home before me and then you disappeared!"

"Don't be stupid. I've just come home and you know it. You heard me ring the bell."

"You have not just come home. I heard you up in the attic and that means you stole the key. I found that key and it was my secret and nobody's allowed to go in my secrets box. And then you went out – you must have done if you've just come in again. And, anyway, when I'm as old as you I'm having a front door key."

"Oh no you're not. Mum doesn't want us to. May has to let us in. And don't you dare tell about May meeting her boyfriend in the afternoons. She's never been more than five minutes late and if you tell I'll kill you."

"I never tell."

"No, but you're so stupid you'll say it by accident and if you do, May will get the sack and go back home to Ireland and then there'll be nobody here when I come home late."

"Oh yes there will! There'll be Marjorie Weaks!"

"There will not, stupid! You know very well Marjorie Weaks only comes to clean twice a week and all the other days there'll be nobody."

James started crying again.

"What have you done to him?" May came back

in and put the biscuits on the table, and held James's head from behind his chair. "Poor little muffin. That's enough, now. Hush."

"She called me stupid," James said.

"Well, she'd no business to do that at all, and you the cleverest boy in your class."

"And she said you'd go away to Ireland."

"Well, I shan't go away to Ireland and that's that."

"May?"

"What? Here, blow your nose." She turned his face up and descended with a handkerchief. James blew. "Hold still now while I wipe your face. You look like the devil himself with the black stripes on you. You're going to have to stop all this howling you do. It's like the wailing of the banshee, do you know that?"

"No!" shouted James, getting his crying muddled up with some laughing. "What's a banshee?"

"It's a terrible old woman in black who wails outside the house where there's a person dying."

James stopped laughing. "Is it a ghost, or what?"

"Yes, May, tell us." Carrie shivered, thinking of the attic. "Is it a ghost? Do you believe in ghosts?"

"What? Is it clanking chains and people with

their heads tucked underneath their arms? I do not! But a twilight ghost, now, that's a different thing altogether."

"A twilight ghost?" Carrie's heart jumped. "What's that? Go on, May, tell. Please."

"No!" shouted James. "I'll get frightened and have nightmares."

"That you will not," said May. "A twilight ghost doesn't come to frighten people, though it might want to tell them something. A twilight ghost is just a kind of long-lost memory that awakens with the last rays of the sun and fades away as the first star comes out and the day dies."

"But what wakens up the memory?" insisted Carrie, thinking of the red reflection in the attic window just before everything went dark and there was no glass, only the black iron bars.

"Somebody switch the light on!" wailed James, but nobody was listening.

"My mother used to say," May began, pouring more tea, and both the children leaned towards her, their eyes wide with interest. Carrie's heart was beating fast. May's mother told her the most amazing things. Perhaps May knew all about the sort of thing that was happening at the attic window.

"What did your mother say?" whispered James.

"She said… It was one summer evening and Mary Theresa – that's my youngest sister – was going to the small meadow to fetch home the geese for the night. Now, geese are terrible creatures to bite and I'll have nothing to do with them myself."

"What did you bite them for, then?" asked James, imagining stiff crunchy feathers in his mouth mixed with the smell of the butcher's shop. "Ugh!"

"She didn't bite them, they bit her," Carrie said. "May says things like that because she comes from Ireland. Now, for goodness' sake, stop interrupting. Go on about the geese, May."

"Well now, the only time I ever brought them home, that divil of a gander got behind me and bit me so hard I didn't sit down for a week. But little Mary Theresa, who was no higher than they were, had them completely under control. They followed her around like ducklings and never once did the gander bite her. He used to eat the corn from her hand. Now, along the path up to the house from the stream beyond the small meadow there's the stump of an old tree. My mother was at the kitchen door that evening having a good old gossip with my Aunty Tess, and I was hanging around listening in, as usual. Mary Theresa came up the path with the geese parading behind her in good military order and when she reached the tree stump she sat down. The geese gathered around her, jostling and murmuring like children waiting for a story. I remember her like it was yesterday though she was no more than six and she turned fourteen this very year. The last rays of the sun glinted red on her soft black curls and the geese themselves looked pink in the sunset. She sat there crooning a little song to them as she fed them corn from her apron pocket."

"What did she sing?" asked James, "to make them good like that?"

"It wasn't the song," May said, "it was herself who understood them. And my mother turned to Aunty Tess and said, 'Look there, Tess,' she said, 'it's poor Kathleen.'"

"You said she was called Mary Theresa," protested James.

"And so she was," said May. "Kathleen was my mother's youngest sister and she died of a fever when she was only twelve."

"What sort of a fever?" asked James.

"Little Kathleen died of the Asian flu. Such an epidemic there was in the fifties."

"Is it worse than the ordinary flu we get?" asked James.

"Much, much worse," said May, "and it killed little Kathleen who would have been my aunty had she lived. 'She was the one who would bring home the geese,' my mother said, watching Mary Theresa and thinking of her own little sister all those years ago, 'and she'd peg down there on that old stump and sing to them as she gave them the corn from her apron pocket. Ah, Tess, it's many an evening of late I've seen her sitting there from my kitchen window. It must be Mary Theresa taking after her that's woken her memory.' And that's when my mother told me about twilight ghosts and how she'd see her little sister sitting on the tree stump with the geese gathered round her in the last rays of the evening sun and how the vision would fade as the first star twinkled in a turquoise sky and the day died."

"And was she sad?" asked Carrie.

"Why should she be sad? She loved her little sister and was glad enough to have her company again for a while."

"But when the vision faded and she was gone again, wasn't she sad then?"

"But she wasn't gone, she was still in my mother's memory. We don't really die until the last person who remembers us dies, and even then, there are other ways of being remembered."

"Like if you're famous," James said. "Dad told me that. I'm going to be famous."

"Oh, shut up," said Carrie. "What other ways are there, May?"

"There's someone coming along in the family later on who takes after you."

"And then does a twilight ghost come?"

"It might do," May said.

"What does 'take after you' mean?" asked James.

"I wish you wouldn't interrupt all the time," Carrie complained. "It means somebody who looks like you. Anybody knows that."

"It means more than that," May said, feeling at the teapot and finding it stone cold. "Remember, Mary Theresa had Kathleen's way with the geese, the same little tricks with them, even sitting on that same tree stump to sing to them. And she took after her in other ways, too. There was nobody could sing the baby to sleep like she could and she was a great one to make pastry. Yet she hadn't been taught those things by Aunt Kathleen – or even seen her do them – because Kathleen died young and none of us children ever knew her."

"Well, who do I take after, then?" asked Carrie.

"And me!" shouted James. "Who do I take after?"

"Oh, you take after your daddy," answered May at once, stroking James's red-blond fringe, "and there's no doubt about that. You'll make a fine engineer when you grow up, for sure."

"I wish he'd come home," James said, and his eyes started filling with tears again. "What does he have to keep going to stupid Hong Kong for?"

"Because," said May, pulling him on to her knee so he wouldn't start crying again, "an important engineer like your daddy has to do big important jobs, and here in England there aren't very many so it's no use wailing like the banshee again."

"Tell us a story, May, then I won't wail, I promise."

"Haven't I your supper to get – and you to bath," threatened May, "and no time at all for such a thing as a story. Not to mention that Carrie, here, hasn't done her homework or been in to say hello to her granny."

"I want to know who I take after," Carrie insisted.

"Not your father," May said, "since you can't do maths, and not your mother, either. She doesn't know a note of music."

"Who then?"

"I don't know at all. Do you have any aunties?"

"No."

"No one you ever heard of in your family with a talent for music?"

"No."

"You'll have to ask your mammy, then, won't you?"

"She's always at work," grumbled Carrie, and she felt like crying just as much as James did. She didn't cry, though, she only went very pale.

"Well," said May, "are we all going to sit here with long faces or is somebody going to decide which story I'm to tell. I can never remember which one it is James likes best, though he's always telling me."

"Michael Jo and Sweeny's Donkey!" shouted James, just like he always did, and May switched on the light and settled down again and everybody felt better. It was nice in the kitchen with the light on and something that smelled good baking in the oven and May telling them stories about Ireland and her favourite brother.

"Can't we have the one about when you found a fairy ring?" Carrie asked.

"No! May, no!"

"I'll tell you the both of them," promised May.

"But Michael Jo and Sweeney's Donkey first!" insisted James. "It all started when your mammy told Michael Jo to go over to Mrs Mannion's with a head of cabbage and he couldn't catch Jack."

"Nobody could catch our Jack," continued May, "because he never came near the house nor the people in it, except at dinnertime when he came braying his head off for the potato water—"

"And Sweeney's donkey lived in your field and he was easy to catch so—"

"Who's telling this story?" asked May.

"You!" shouted James, his eyes bright and his face pink with all the laughter that was ready to explode inside him when Michael Jo got thrown into the ditch head first again.

When Michael Jo and Sweeny's Donkey and Finding the Fairy Ring had both been told, May said, "Listen, now, I've thought of a treat. I'm making us a grand supper. I've most of it in the oven already, a chicken pie and baked potatoes. I've just a fine big green salad to dress."

"Great!" shouted James.

"Wait a minute, will you? That's not the treat, that's just your supper. The treat is: if you're bathed and in your pyjamas, James, and if Carrie's done her homework and you've both been in to see your granny, you can stay up till your mammy gets back from the hospital and have your supper with her. She'll not mind just the once to cheer you up."

"Great!" said James, "and I've been in to see Gran already."

"Right," said May. "Let me check the oven and I'll bath you. Carrie, off you go to see your granny."

"I'll go after," Carrie said.

"After what?"

"After."

"Come on, now. The poor soul sees nobody all day but me, stuck in there with that blessed television on from morning till night."

"Well, why can't she sit in here with us? It's so gloomy in her room with all those mouldy old books and all those photographs of people we don't know."

"They're all the company she has, poor soul, and she can't sit with us in here, which she'd love to do more than anything, because, in case you haven't noticed, she's in a wheelchair which won't come down those stairs since wheelchairs haven't wings. Now, off you go — and thank her for your new trainers — or do you not want to stay up?"

Carrie just couldn't stand the thought of her

gran shut up all day in that room in her wheelchair. Every time she went in there she would lie awake in bed afterwards, thinking of gran the way she used to be, always making something, cakes and pies, curtains, cushion covers and new dresses for Carrie. Now she couldn't even walk and her hand... her poor hand that couldn't move at all...

Carrie turned her face away, "All right, I'll go when I've done my homework."

"That's what you said last night, or am I mistaken?"

"I've said I'll go!"

"All right, all right. No need to shout."

So May checked the oven and they all set off up the stairs together. When Carrie stopped outside grandma's room, James said, "May? Carrie's been looking in my secrets box and she's taken the key to the attic stairs door that I found by myself and she's not supposed to go in my box, Mum said."

"I haven't been in your stupid box and I haven't been up in the attic!" Carrie stood outside her gran's door watching them go on up the stairs.

She heard James say, "You won't leave me by myself when I'm in the bath, will you, May?" He was scared of the stained glass window on the landing because it reflected strange coloured shapes on the walls that he said were red–hot ghosts.

When they were nearly at the top she heard him say, "Now you have to hold my hand." And then he said, "Carrie did go up in the attic, May. I heard her up there when I came in from school. She was playing her flute. Nobody else plays the flute, do they, May? So it must have been her."

⭑ CHAPTER THREE ⭑

"HELLO, SWEETHEART! ARE you going to have five minutes with me?"

The minute Carrie walked into her grandmother's room she felt her heart ache with guilty sadness. The trouble was that the longer she avoided her gran, the heavier the sadness would become, so that she would put off having to face it for even longer.

Gran was sitting in her wheelchair parked in front of the television which was switched on without the sound. Perhaps she kept it on even when there was nothing she wanted to watch so she wouldn't feel lonely. This was one of the rooms with bay windows which you could see from the street but, despite the big window, it always seemed rather gloomy and Gran kept a lamp lit on the long sideboard, next to the silver tray where there were always sweets for Carrie and James.

"Come and sit down, then," Gran said. "Push Bess off that chair. I don't want her jumping up on the table. Now then, tell me what you've been up to. You look upset. Are you all right?"

"Of course I am, Gran, and I haven't been doing anything interesting, only school and boring stuff." She put the fat grey cat down on the floor and sat down on the warm chair. "What have you been up to?"

Carrie said that because she didn't want to talk about herself but the minute the words were out she realised what a stupid question she'd asked. What could her gran have been up to except sitting in that horrible wheelchair in this same room, day after long boring day. How did she stand it?

"Oh, I'm all right. Don't worry about me," she said, as if she could read Carrie's mind.

Carrie leaned her elbows on the big polished

table, cupping her chin in her hands. "Don't you get bored?"

"No," Gran said. "I know it seems strange to you, but when you get old, you start living more inside your head than in the world around you. You even find yourself having a chat in your head with someone who's long dead, like my Jim – your grandad, you know – or... well, your father, even though he's away. You know them so well, you see, that you can imagine their side of the conversation and you know what advice they'd give you if you have a problem. You never lose your real friends. You're too young to have friends like that yet but little Katy would be one, I think. That's a very special little girl, you know. I hope you'll always stay friends. D'you remember your white frocks with the velvet flocking?"

"Our Easter dresses!?"

"You still remember? You were only six, both of you. That was a remnant from my man at the market. I got it for a song. Fancy you remembering."

"It was the feel of the stuff more than anything. I can still feel it now, that soft muslin and the tiny flecks of white velvet, just like snowflakes. And having them the same, that was the best thing of all! We used to pretend to be twins, do you remember?"

"I don't remember that but I do remember your long plaits and how you always had your heads together, giggling and whispering… and what thin little legs – you were like two swans in those white muslin frocks – how that child's face lit up when she saw there was one for her, too. How is she getting on with her dancing?"

"All right."

Gran laughed. "I'm sorry," she said, "I shouldn't laugh and I shouldn't ask you questions. It's a bad habit grown-ups have, isn't it? I even do it to poor little James and he says school's all right and he's all right and living in this house is all right. Then I have to decide, according to exactly how he says 'all right', what the real answer is. And the real answer to how does he like living in this house is that he doesn't. I think he hates it."

Carrie was embarrassed. After all, it was Gran's house. She didn't want to offend her so she changed the subject, saying, "Can I have a sweet from the tray?"

"Of course you can. They're the honey ones that you like. And I suppose, since you've changed the subject, that you hate living here, too."

Carrie went to the sideboard to get her sweet, keeping her red face hidden from Gran.

"James is still upset because he had to leave all his friends in Sharwood Avenue and he's frightened of all the dark places in this house because he's only seven."

"And what are you frightened of? You're eleven. I think if I were eleven I'd find it depressing living with an old lady in a wheelchair. It's an ugly thing, isn't it? I hate it myself – but I'm learning to walk, you know. I'll surprise you one day. You'll come in and find me up in the kitchen making a one-handed pie, you mark my words. Then you won't have to see this depressing thing again."

"Oh, Gran, I'm sorry! It isn't like that, it isn't!" Carrie ran back to Gran and hugged her, still trying to hide her face.

"Now, now, what's all this?" Gran took Carrie by the shoulders and held her away so she could see her face. "You're crying. Carrie, listen to me. You've been unhappy ever since you came to live here. Do you think I haven't noticed? You're pale and you're cross and I never hear you play your flute. I remember the cheerful little chatterbox who used to play cards with me when her daddy brought her along to keep me company when he came to sort out my papers and bills. Do you remember? You loved playing cards but, more than

anything, you loved rummaging in the top drawer
of the sideboard, playing at being a grown-up lady
with my old powder compacts and beads and
forgotten bottles of scent."

"And those gloves," Carrie said. "A pair of white
kid gloves. I always put those on."

"That's right, you did. And now it's little James
who comes to play in the drawer with your
grandad's old things. He pins lots of war medals on
and pretends to be a general in charge of a space
mission to Mars."

"What did grandad get his medals for? Was he in
the war? Was he brave?"

"He was very brave – but not in the last war. He
was in his forties then and too old to go and fight.
He was a lot older than me, you see, even though
I'm a hundred and ten."

"You're not a hundred and ten!"

"All right," Gran said, laughing, "but your
grandad was eighty-six when he died and that's ten
years ago. He got his medals fighting in the
trenches in the First World War. I don't think he
ever got over it. He and his friends volunteered,
you see, and they were all killed except him. He
was a wonderful man, your grandad. Gentle and
patient, never wanting or expecting anything for

himself, but he was always a bit sad. I loved him very much but I was never able to touch that sadness and I often thought it must have been the war that caused it. All his friends were killed. The one and only time I felt something really made him feel better was when you were born. That changed him. He'd always wanted a daughter, you see, but after your father was born I was never able to have any more children. Oh he did so want a little girl. There's a nursery, you know, on the top floor of this house and he had everything done up when I was expecting, all ready for a girl, even to the pink ribbons on his own old cradle. Then your daddy was born. He never said anything but he was very disappointed, I know."

"And did Dad have to sleep in the cradle with the pink ribbons?"

"No, of course not. When he turned out to be a boy all that was forgotten. Anyway, attic nurseries had gone out of fashion by then for people like us who couldn't afford a full-time nurse. I couldn't be running up and down that staircase. Your father slept in a new cot by my bed. Then, when he was big enough, I put him in the room little James has now."

Remembering, Carrie said, "James says he's found the key to the attic stairs door."

"And so he did. It was in the cigar box with Grandad's medals."

Carrie was quiet for a moment, staring at the silently-moving figures on the television screen, thinking about that key and the terror of the attic window.

"What is it, Carrie?" Gran stroked her long hair gently. "What's upsetting you? Is it just growing up that's hard?"

"No. It's nothing – oh, Gran, it's everything. It's Dad being away and Mum always out at work, and I did love our own house – it's not because of you, Gran, honestly – I liked it because it was light and cheerful and new, and I'm sick of school, as well, and I hate practising the flute and—"

"That's enough! Woah! We can't solve all those problems at once. You've got to separate them."

"What do you mean?"

"When you have a long list of problems like that you must look at them one by one and then you'll find that only one of them is really a problem and all the rest is just what I call grumble jumble."

"What's that? Grumbling?"

"Oh no, it's quite different. Grumbling's wicked, whining about things instead of getting on with them cheerfully when they've got to be done.

Grumble jumble's quite another thing. It happens when something's really upsetting you but you don't quite understand it so you blame everything else instead because when you're unhappy, you're unhappy in everything you do. Once you've decided what the real problem is, you can start to solve it and all the rest, the grumble jumble, disappears like snow in sunshine and there's nothing there at all. Do you understand?"

"I think I do, a bit."

"Well, a bit will do for now. We can get started with a bit. Now then: school, the flute, your parents, this house… A lot of those are connected, aren't they? Your mummy and daddy had to sell their house and move in with me because the firm your daddy worked for closed down. Then there was no work for him in England, so he went abroad by himself so as not to disturb you too much, and your mummy went back to work to help a bit with money, so that sometime you can have another new house of your own. So, all those things are just about your daddy losing his job, aren't they?"

"I know, but it's horrible that he only comes home for a few days every so often!"

"It's much worse for him than it is for you. You

have little James and your mummy and May and me near you, and we all love you."

"James doesn't."

"Yes, he does. He doesn't know he does but he does. Your daddy, though, he's far away from everyone who loves him, remember that. Now then, what about this house? Why is it so terrible?"

"Oh…" She couldn't tell the truth about what she'd seen. She hadn't even told May who believed in twilight ghosts.

"You don't need to be afraid of offending me. It isn't my house, not the way you think. Your grandad brought me here when he married me after the war. He was so much older, forty-four, and I was just a silly young girl. Oh, how I hated this gloomy old house! But Jim was trying to build up his business and we couldn't afford a new house."

"You could have sold this one."

"Not in those days. They're back in fashion now and people divide them up into flats but then nobody wanted these great rambling ugly houses, they wanted nice new modern ones that you could run without help. And then, you know, your grandad was born here and perhaps he wanted to stay and fill up the nursery with happy children."

'But you didn't like it here."

"No, and I couldn't really understand why he was so insistent on staying but he was a good man, Carrie, and I loved him very much. When you really love somebody you do things for them without understanding. Even so, I wish I had been able to understand. He was a very secretive man in many ways and there were some things in his life he never talked about even to me. What a pity it is that he didn't live long enough for you to know him. His little Edwina! He chose your first name, you know, though you've never used it."

"Oh Gran, nobody's called Edwina – and, anyway, I'm called Edwina Caroline Grey, and Caroline's after you so Carrie's better."

"Well," Gran smiled. "I suppose it doesn't matter. As long as my Jim was alive he was able to think of you as Edwina. There he is looking at us. He was so handsome in his uniform."

Carrie gazed across at he masses of photos in silver frames on the table next to the fireplace. Those photos, many of them brown and faded, had always made her feel sad but today she felt curious about the people in them.

"He is handsome," she said. "Gran, do I take after any of those people? Do I take after Grandad?"

"Oh no no, I don't think so. He was an engineer, you know, like your father and like your great-grandfather. You must take after somebody musical but I can't think who it could be…"

"But Grandad left me his flute!" Carrie remembered suddenly. "Dad told me when he gave it to me on my eighth birthday. You remember, don't you?"

"I do remember," Gran said, "but I think the flute must have belonged to someone else in the family because it wasn't his. He couldn't play it. Perhaps it belonged to his mother or one of her sisters. There they are, look, all four together with their mother. The Hoyle girls… what beauties they were with their tiny waists and lacy blouses. Now, you do have a look of my Jim's mother, so perhaps that's the answer."

Carrie jumped up from her chair to get the photograph and take a closer look.

"Draw the curtains first, there's a good girl," Gran said, "and switch the big lamp on so we'll be cosy."

As she pulled the heavy velvet curtains, the fat grey cat jumped down from the windowsill. Carrie looked out at the huge black houses in the dark street and shivered at the thought of the barred window high above this one. She turned back quickly to switch on the cheerful light, get the photograph and settle down on the rug at Gran's feet.

"Ah, the Hoyle girls…" Gran took the picture from Carrie and studied it. "Your grandad always kept this photo by him. 'They were all beautiful, Caroline,' he used to say, 'but my mother was the most beautiful of them all.' And it's true, isn't it? There she is in the middle: Margaret. And the others are Mary, Lucy and Ellen. This is their mother, Emily. Margaret died before I met your grandad so I never knew her. The story is she died of a broken heart – they used to say that in the old days. Nobody says it any more but it's true that a very great sorrow can damage your health beyond repair."

"And what was her great sorrow?" Carrie asked, looking at the sweet face under the heavy coils of hair, piled high and held with a black satin bow.

"I don't remember that your grandad ever told me," Gran said.

"But do I take after her?" Carrie insisted. "Do I look like her a bit?"

"Wait a minute," Gran said, "and give me my glasses – there they are on the table where you were leaning before… thank you. Mm… You do have a look of her, mostly about the eyes. You get those eyes from your father and he got them from his grandmother, Margaret. Still, it's not a very striking likeness and we don't know that she was musical."

Carrie knelt up to take a closer look. "I wish I looked more like her. She's so pretty with that little rosebud mouth and that high lace collar – and look at her hair, Gran! Would my hair go up like that? Mine's long enough but hers is so thick and puffy."

"Don't you believe it. My mother told me that they used to wind their own hair round thick pads of real hair that you could buy."

"Real hair? You mean somebody else's hair? Ugh! I wouldn't fancy that. And what about this one? She has her hair down. Why?"

"That's Lucy, the youngest. Young ladies used to put their hair up when they were grown up and ready to be married. What a shame we don't know if your flute was Margaret's. Of course, all young ladies used to play music in those days – usually the piano – and sing, too. A lot of them did it very badly but they had to do it anyway. There was no television to pass the time on long winter evenings, so the girls of the family had to entertain everybody."

"What about the boys?"

"Oh, they'd join in the singing sometimes but they weren't expected to play."

"That's not fair! I wouldn't have stood for that if it had been me."

"You would, you know," said Gran, laughing, "because you wouldn't have thought it strange that girls and boys had different lives. You might have been glad of it when there was a war and the boys had to go, no matter how frightened they were."

But Carrie wasn't listening. She was piling her hair on top of her head and trying to look like Margaret but it all tumbled down again and she couldn't squash her lips into a little rosebud shape either.

"Oh Gran, don't I take after anybody?" she asked, looking across at the rest of the photographs.

"Nobody I can think of," Gran said. "Why are you so interested, all of a sudden? Most children hate that sort of thing. I always do my best to remember never to make comments on how much they've grown or who they look like."

"I know, but May said…"

'What did May say?"

"Oh… nothing. May's great, isn't she, Gran?"

"She's a good-hearted girl, and great company for me."

"I know. She is for us, as well. Gran, will you try and think who I take after? I can't tell you why. It's a secret and I can't explain it."

"Have you forgotten already what I told you about your grandad and me? When you love somebody you do things for them even without understanding. You keep your secret and I'll do my best to tell you what you want to know. All right?"

"Oh Gran, you're so nice! You're not a bit like other grown–ups." Carrie knelt up again to hug her.

"Don't get soppy!" Gran said, hugging her back. "I'll dig out your grandad's old photograph albums and we'll find out who you take after if it's the last thing we do!"

Gran was great. She was never annoyed if you didn't go in and see her very often. She never said she was too busy or too tired to help you. She always took you seriously when you had a problem and always made you laugh when you were sad.

Carrie thought of all those things and said, "All right."

Another good thing about Gran was that she always kept her promises but she wasn't going to be able to keep this one because Carrie decided right then that she was going to steal the key to the attic stairs door from James's secrets box. And once she went up there it would be too late.

~ CHAPTER FOUR ~

THE SECRETS IN James's box were not very exciting for anybody except James himself. The only thing he kept there that Carrie liked, was a big amethyst still embedded in the piece of rock it had been cut from. A geologist friend of their father's had given it to James on his birthday. There was also a tiny magnifying glass set on a spiral wire stand and three very pretty stamps which had been meant as the beginning of a stamp collection that had never got any bigger. All the other things in the box were junk: a seaside pebble, a story cut out of his favourite comic and stuck with sticky tape into one long strip, a magazine advert for a mountain bike he wanted when he was big enough, some plaited coloured string and a few foreign coins. What rubbish it all was and how stupid boys were, Carrie thought as she poked about looking for the key. She was trying to hide from how guilty she felt about opening his precious box.

She'd had to wait until Thursday afternoon to get at it. May had taken James to the dentist straight after school. She found the key buried underneath all the other things, perhaps because he thought she'd taken it out and used it the other day. It was all wrapped up in pages from his comic and wound round with lots of sticky tape. She would have to wrap it up again afterwards, she decided, dropping the screwed-up paper on James's bed and going off with the key.

The door to the attic stairs was at the end of the corridor where their two bedrooms were. It wasn't difficult to open with the small iron key but when Carrie pressed the light switch at the bottom of the staircase, nothing happened. The bulb must have gone. Her heart began pounding fast. It was only about five in the afternoon, it was true, but the day was rainy and dark and, in any case, the attic window had always done its strange tricks in the twilight.

"I'm not scared!" she said loudly. The words seemed to hang in the air of the empty house so that she went on hearing them like an echo.

"I'm not scared."

"I'm not scared!"

But the echo voice didn't sound at all like her own voice. She looked up at the dark and narrow staircase and placed her right hand carefully on the thin, polished bannister.

"I'll just go up to the top and come straight down again if I don't like it."

More words that hung in the air with the others.

A stair creaked loudly, making her jump.

"I'm not scared!"

"I'm not..." She started to climb the bare wooden stairs, sniffing the strange musty smell. She was wearing her new white trainers so her footsteps were quiet enough but then she trod on a stair that creaked loudly, making her jump. At the top she stopped. She could hear the rain gurgling in the leaky troughing and then a car swishing past outside. A nice ordinary noise. There was a corridor like the one on the floor below but the first door had been taken off. Around the empty doorway was some cement and plaster work and most of the old flowery wallpaper had been stripped away from the whole corridor. This must have been part of Grandad's attempt at doing up the attic when Carrie's father was born and he'd given up without finishing because the baby wasn't a girl. The room beyond was gloomy but Carrie could see nothing in there that looked at all frightening so she went in. The rain was pouring down so hard outside the dirty, barred window that you could smell its wetness in the room. At once, Carrie looked about for the cradle with pink bows on it but there wasn't one. Perhaps it had been thrown away. There was more bare plaster on the inside of the doorway and a bucket stood on a wooden table in the centre of the room. There was another table against the wall and standing on that were a huge jug and basin, white with blue flowers. Next to this table was a little polished wooden stand of some sort with three fancy rails. Carrie didn't know what it could be for but, anyway, somebody had left a long strip of torn wallpaper draped over it. Her heartbeat slowed down to normal. There was nothing frightening up here at all. She must have imagined all that stuff about the window. Perhaps she'd had a nervous breakdown. She knew all about nervous breakdowns from May whose Aunty Bridget had once had one and, as a consequence of "seeing things", "had to be taken away". Carrie stopped feeling frightened and started feeling disappointed. Then she noticed a big green cupboard and felt hopeful again. The door creaked dreadfully as she opened it and she shivered at the noise. Inside were shelves, stacked mostly with towels and sheets, which had once been white but were now yellowy and blackened along their folds. In the corner of one shelf were lots of bars of soap wrapped in dirty yellow paper. Carrie picked one up. The yellow paper was thick and rough. She sniffed at it.

"Ugh!" Carrie threw it back in the cupboard. "That's horrible... it stinks!" She shut the doors of the boring, nasty-smelling cupboard and went over to the window to look down at the rain splashing into the darkened street and think about how she had stood there in front of the black house opposite, staring up in terror at the spot where she was standing now. The glass was filthy, covered with a thick layer of dust. When she reached out her hand to see if it was on the inside or the outside she saw that her hand was already black, probably from touching the dirty packets of soap. She pulled a tissue out of the pocket of her jeans and wiped her hands clean as best she could. Underneath the dirt they were red and blue with cold.

"It's freezing up here." It was damp, too. Again she noticed the smell of the dirty city rain as strong as if it were raining indoors.

She thought she might as well look next door. You didn't have to go out and along the corridor like you did on the floor below because there was a little door in the wall between the two rooms.

"Ah…" This was more like it. The first thing she spotted was the cradle with its muslin curtains and dusty pink satin bows. The wallpaper had nursery rhymes with pictures all over it. She saw Little Miss Muffet and Little Jack Horner and Mary, Mary, Quite Contrary and Hickory Dickory Dock repeated over and over again. But in the corner, where the roof sloped down near the window, the paper was wet and sagging and some of it was trailing on the floor.

"So it is raining indoors." Outside, the broken troughing gurgled and spouted as the rain came down harder and harder and found its way in to dribble down the mouldy wall. Carrie picked up the trail of sodden nursery rhyme paper and it fell to pieces.

"A toy box!" Carrie pushed the rest of the paper away. There it was, standing in the corner. You could tell because it was painted green with pictures of a soldier and a drum and a harlequin. Carrie crouched down and opened the lid, forgetting all about Grandad and twilight ghosts in the joy of discovering treasure. There were three single beds in the room and she began pulling out toys and spreading them on the dusty counterpane of the nearest one. She considered herself far too old for toys, of course, but this was different. These were really old toys, probably antiques, and worth lots of money. She found a drum rather like the one painted on the box, red and blue and silver with red and blue tassels and wooden drumsticks. Then she pulled out a tambourine with a dancing gypsy girl painted on it and faded yellow ribbons. There was a tiny Punch and Judy theatre with a handle to turn that made the figures move and played a brief tinny tune. One thing she put aside carefully on another bed for herself and that was a pretty blue velvet box with a silver tassel on it. Like many of the toys, it had been a bit spoiled by rainwater seeping into the toy box, so that on one side the velvet was wet and the colour faded.

Still, she thought, she could put it on her

dressing table with the faded side at the back and keep her watch and bangles in it. There was even a tiny key in the keyhole at the front. She turned it and pulled. Out came a miniature drawer lined with satin which, as Carrie had imagined, was for keeping trinkets in. There on the white satin lay a silver chain and locket.

"Oh! I'm keeping it – please let me keep it!" Carrie said to nobody at all. She took the locket and opened it. There were photographs in each side, a man's head and a woman's, browny yellowy photos like the ones in Gran's room. What's more, the lady looked like Margaret. You could see, even on such a small picture, that she had a rosebud mouth and puffed-up hair and a high frill around her chin. Carrie put the locket and chain around her neck and fastened it. She would show that to Gran, but first she wanted to see what other treasure was in the box. She knelt down again and carried on pulling things out. She tooted on a brass trumpet and wondered if anybody would ever get a minute's peace again if she gave that and the drum to James. She found a Noah's ark and a wooden stand with holes for pegs to be knocked through with a mallet. Then she found something else she wanted to keep because, even if she was too old for it, it really was pretty: a cardboard doll with cut-out paper dresses and hats in the same style as the beautiful, frilly clothes in the photo of the Hoyle girls. There was even a cardboard wardrobe, covered with brown leatherette and with a little row of hooks inside to hang the frocks and a drawer at the bottom for hats. She had got to the bottom of the toy box now and there was nothing much left except a mouldy leather-bound book and a jumble of wooden bricks and chalks and broken lead soldiers. She opened the book to see if it looked worth reading but it wasn't a story book at all, it was a diary. On the flyleaf, in spidery brown writing was written:

James Edward Grey
1918

"Grandad Grey…" Carrie said. She tried to read a bit of it but the diary had been lying at the bottom of the box in the wettest corner. Its brown leather cover was covered in green mould and the handwriting on every page had been partly obliterated by a big brown patch of wetness. As she flicked the pages, a photograph fell on to the bed. Carrie examined it. She recognised Grandad Grey at once from the picture of him in Gran's room.

The other three must have been the friends he went to the war with and whose deaths had made him sad for the rest of his life.

"They all look quite handsome," Carrie thought aloud, "but none of them is as handsome as Grandad Grey." It was only possible to read the top few lines of each page of the diary, the part above the brown patch.

16th January.

Jack died last night. His wound was very slight, a bullet that barely grazed him, and he joked about his good fortune at its being his foot. The bandages meant he couldn't get his boot on and so he could be sent down to base and take it easy for a day or two. Then came the infection and a fever and now he's gone. We lied about our ages. He was eighteen today

The rest of the page had gone. She looked at some more legible bits but they only talked about the war and she couldn't understand them. Then there was something about the weather that didn't look at all interesting. How could he think about the weather in a war with people firing guns and his best friends dying?

It began to snow last night when I was on sentry duty. Before that the cold made your bones ache but then the air seemed kinder. Snow is so quiet and soft it calms the spirit. I came here to die because of what I did long ago but perhaps my duty is to live. The quietness of snow. The quietness of acceptance

Oh, why were there never more than six lines you could read? Whatever could Grandad Grey have done that was so terrible? She tried the next page and found something about a nightmare:

and again last night. They say I keep repeating that I can't go by myself and that I try to cover my head with anything I can find. Of course they think I'm afraid which is only natural. I can't tell them what I did but I understand now that just as I broke my mother's heart, then it will kill my father if I die out here and I know I shall be left alive to return to Stoneleigh and find some other way to atone

The next readable page was about two horses drowning and not about himself at all. Suddenly she heard little James's voice shrieking above the noise of the rain. She dashed to the window with the diary still in her hands and looked down. James was splashing furiously through all the puddles towards home in his bright yellow oilskin mac and sou'wester. He loved the rain and leapt in and out of each puddle two or three times, sending up spray with his red wellingtons. May was hurrying along behind him, huddled under her umbrella. Only when May was fumbling in her shoulder bag for the key did Carrie remember. The key! She ran to the door but ran back again for her velvet box, then hurtled down the stairs and, with no time to relock the door, pushed the key back in its wrapping and into the box and under James's bed.

"Carrie!" That was May. "Are you there?"

"Coming!" She ran to her own room with the little box and the diary and then started downstairs. She was in such a hurry that she didn't see the photograph that fell to the floor by her bed.

By the time she reached the kitchen she had got her breath back. James had just had a brace put on his huge new front teeth and his mouth was firmly shut as he sat on the kitchen floor pulling at his wellingtons.

"Will I help you with those?" asked May.

"I can do it myself," growled James out of the corner of his mouth. "Tell Carrie she hasn't to laugh at me!"

"Sure, she'd a brace on her teeth herself at your age. Why should she laugh?"

Carrie opened her mouth to say I did not, but she saw May wink at her just in time and kept quiet.

"Was it the same as mine?" James asked the question with his mouth still pretty well closed so that it sounded more like *Os it er sane as nine?*

"Just the very same and why wouldn't it be? Now put your slippers on and let's all have a nice cup of tea."

Poor James kept his mouth shut for the rest of the evening, even while he was chewing his food, something nobody had managed to convince him to do before.

When Carrie passed his door on her way to bed he called in a loud whisper:

"*Carrie!*"

"What do you want?" She could barely see him at all when she went in. He had the sheet pulled up to his nose and his freckles and fringe were pink in the glow of his red night-light.

"You haven't to tell anybody at school about my brace. Promise."

"Don't be stupid, they'll see it for themselves."

"They won't because I'm going to keep my mouth shut all the time. I haven't got buck teeth."

"I know you haven't. For goodness' sake, Mum spent hours explaining to you about your jaw being slightly bigger at the top than at the bottom. Nobody's ever said you had buck teeth."

"Well, I haven't and you have to promise not to tell at school."

"Well… all right, but you have to give me the key to the attic stairs door so I can go up and see… if there are any toys there. It was Grandad Grey's nursery so there might be."

"All right, but you have to promise first."

"I promise."

"Cross your heart and hope to die."

"Cross my heart and hope to die."

James hung out of bed and fished for his precious box. With only the night-light on he didn't notice how carelessly the key was wrapped in its bit of comic and he gave it up to Carrie without another word. She felt a bit guilty – after all he was only little – so she said, "If there are some good toys I'll bring you something down – or else you could come up with me, if you want."

"Are there any red-hot ghosts up there?"

"Of course not."

"There might be. I'm only coming if May comes as well."

Carrie left him and went to her own room. When she was ready for bed she took off her watch, thinking she could put it in the drawer of the blue velvet box. But the watch was a big clumsy plastic one and wouldn't fit in the tiny drawer at all so she took off the locket and put that in instead, along with the attic door key.

"I'll keep it here next to my lamp on the dressing table," she said to herself, and she lifted the velvet box by its silk tassel. Except that the box didn't lift up, only the top did. As it opened, a tiny ballerina came up on a satin-covered pedestal, as if by magic, and a tune began to play as the dancer turned slowly on one toe. A round mirror below the pedestal reflected her dance.

"A musical jewellery box!" Carrie had never seen such a lovely thing before. The ballerina was made of porcelain and when Carrie peered more closely at it she exclaimed, "But it looks just like Katy!" The moment she said it the ballerina and the music stopped dead. Carrie knew that a music box shouldn't stop like that. It ought to wind down gradually because it was clockwork. Perhaps it was broken. She shut the box carefully and searched its base until she found the key that wound it up.

"Oh no!" She had wound it as far as she could and pulled the tassel, but the music wouldn't start or the ballerina dance. It seemed likely that water had got into the mechanism and caused it to rust. Carrie got in bed and snapped her light off angrily. She really was very disappointed. It was a long time before she calmed down enough to realise that it could probably be mended and that Gran would be just the person to ask. And it was an even longer time – in fact she was practically asleep – before she suddenly opened her eyes wide and asked herself the obvious question: if that was Grandad Grey's room, why was there a jewellery box and paper dolls?

‑CHAPTER FIVE‑

FRIDAY WAS A grey and empty day. In the afternoon, dirty clouds were being blown across the sky by a cold, unfriendly wind. Carrie felt so lonely she'd have done anything to stop Katy leaving her and going straight home. She wanted them both to go with Sophie's gang, who always hung out around the centre after school and, on Fridays, had a pizza together at a new place that had opened. They were mostly older than Carrie and Katy but one of them, a big, red-haired girl called Annette, was in their class and had suggested she should go with them.

"Oh come on, Katy, don't be such a spoilsport."

"I'm not being a spoilsport," Katy said, "I'm not stopping you going with them." And she started walking away from the school gate, tramping through the ruffled leaves with her head down. She was right, of course. It was just that, if she didn't come too, Carrie couldn't pretend to think it was all right. It wasn't all right and she knew it. Besides, she was a bit scared of the older girls and the things she'd heard about them. You couldn't stay a little kid for ever, though, could you? Just now she wished she were a kid and that she and Katy were going home together to lie on Katy's lumpy old bed, giggling and whispering secrets, and then going down to eat sausage and mash and watch children's television. But they were too old for that now. Anyway, Annette had a boyfriend – or said she had – and she said there was a boy from Albert Road Comprehensive who liked Carrie. That made Carrie feel excited but really scared, as well, because of things she'd heard about Sophie's gang. The trouble was, she was even more scared of going home. This morning, looking with pleasure at the little velvet box on the chest by her bed, she thought that it would be different now. After all, she'd been up in the attic and seen nothing frightening there. But then she spotted, half under the bed, near her new white trainers, the old brown photograph that had fallen there yesterday.

"It must have been in the diary..." There was nowhere else it could have come from. It was the photograph of a little girl. She was wearing a white sailor suit and had a big floppy bow in her long loose hair. She seemed to be sitting on some sort of box or stool with a huge fur rug draped over it and her feet were bare.

"It's you, then," said Carrie softly to the solemn little face in the picture. "It's your music box and they're your paper dolls. But who are you?" She turned the photograph over to see if there was anything written on it and was surprised to find that it had been printed as a postcard. It hadn't been sent to anybody because there was no stamp or address or message on it but somebody had written across it diagonally:

Edwina aged 5.

Edwina. Edwina who? Whoever the girl was, one thing was certain: even though she was so much younger, there was no mistaking that she looked just like Carrie.

"Are you why I'm called Edwina?" wondered Carrie. "Why Grandad Grey chose that name for me? You are. You're the girl at the window and I thought I recognised you because you look like me. It's you. You're my twilight ghost.

Now it was time to go home she found that it wasn't different at all. If anything, now she'd been in the attic it was worse. Just the thought of Stoneleigh and the white figure at the barred attic window made her feel sweaty and sick. She felt that if she went back there something dreadful would happen. The image of the tall black house filled her head so that she couldn't think straight. All she could do was to go on uselessly tormenting her friend. She couldn't say "Please don't leave me alone, I'm scared," so she said, "Why do you have to be such a wet? It's only a pizza. It's only for an hour!"

"My gran would call the police if I were an hour late coming home from school. Anyway, I have to shop for her on Fridays."

"You can do it tomorrow."

Katy tramped on, her small face even whiter than usual, her dark brown plait swinging. "Go with them."

They were there on the opposite corner now, giggling and chattering. When she saw Annette looking across at her, Carrie moved slightly away from Katy. Sophie's gang had the trendiest hairdos in the school – the Head had sent them home more than once – and poor Katy with her tight plait was so tidy and old-fashioned. Carrie used to torment her about the way she looked until that awful business of the shoes. Last January, Katy's gran had given her money to get some shoes and Carrie had gone with her to buy them.

"Katy, look! Look at these, they're brilliant!"

"I can't buy those. My gran…"

"They're not for your gran, they're for you. Come on, Katy, they're really great! Annette's got the red ones."

"I've got to get something I can wear for school…"

"So get the black ones and I'll ask my mum if I can get them as well."

"I don't—"

"They're practically half price!"

Even the shop assistant seemed dubious and gave Carrie a funny look, saying that sale goods couldn't be exchanged. Katy put the shoes on with her school uniform, looked ridiculous, and was sent home by the Head, red-faced and in tears. All through the winter she came to school in her old shoes that let water in. There had been no more whispering and giggling on Katy's lumpy old bed.

They both pretended it was because Carrie had moved further away.

Perhaps Katy, too, was remembering the shoe business because she showed no signs of relenting and letting Carrie get her into trouble today. She flung the ends of her striped scarf over her shoulder and walked faster.

"If it's because you have no money, I'll pay for you." Carrie had three weeks' flute lesson money in her pocket. If she got found out it was just too bad.

"It's not because I've no money."

"Of course it is. You never have any money!"

Why was she doing it? The more miserable she felt, the nearer the moment when she had to decide what to do, the more she attacked Katy. Attacked everything about Katy that distressed her, like her old-fashioned clothes, her having no parents, her poverty.

"You'd better go, if you're going."

"I want you to come. I can't stand it when you're like this."

They were at the corner of Katy's street by now and Carrie stopped. Katy turned right and went on without saying anything. Carrie stood watching her as she disappeared into the poky terraced house halfway along the short street. Even then she still stood there, remembering herself rattling the letter box and charging in at Katy's door. She used to run here across the fields behind the church at the bottom end in those days when she lived in Sharwood Avenue. For her it had just been Katy's street and she had never noticed how poor and ugly it was. There were no fallen leaves here. The wind was shuffling some screwed-up newspaper and food-stained wrappers about. The door of St Paul's was boarded over and behind its black spire an ugly, red block of flats showed against the ragged cloudy sky. The wind blew irritatingly this way and that and Carrie felt raindrops on it. She shivered and, all of a sudden, Stoneleigh rose, black and frightening in her mind until she couldn't think of anything else.

She turned and ran, keeping her eyes half shut, trying in this stupid way not to see what was inside her head, to blot it out before the white figure appeared.

"Hey! Carrie!" It was Sophie's gang and Annette was shouting to her. "Are you coming or not?"

"I'm coming!" She stopped dead and then crossed over slowly, trying not to let it show how out of breath she was. "I just had to lend Katy Fishwick a fiver. She's really hard up." Nobody took any notice of what she'd said. It was a stupid story to invent but she was embarrassed and angry with Katy for not staying with her. They drifted on towards the gang's usual corner opposite the supermarket.

Half an hour later they were still there, hanging around outside the pizza place, and they had been joined by a group of boys from Albert Road Comprehensive. Nobody spoke a word to Carrie. She leaned against the wall and tried to look as if she were bored with having such a good time and tired of the conversation which had never included her and which she didn't even understand. She pulled her loose hair forward at each side of her face and turned the collar of her school mac up. She thought she looked at least fifteen. She was growing more and more scared about how late it was getting and her feet were cold. At last somebody said, "Are we going in or what?" and they started pushing in through the double glass doors. A waft of hot dough and onions met them. Some of the boys, much bigger and older than Carrie, barged past her so that she lost her balance. Now she felt more like five than fifteen and Katy's words kept going through her head: *"My gran would call the police if I were an hour late."* Would May call the police? She wasn't the type to panic… Then Carrie remembered that her mother was on the morning shift. She had been up and gone before Carrie and James came downstairs and would be at home by now. How could she have forgotten? Her heart beat louder and faster but she didn't know how to get away. How could she say "I've got to go home or else my mum might call the police." She would sound like Katy. It was impossible. Everybody was still standing around because there wasn't a free table big enough for all of them. She found herself near red-haired Annette who said something to her. Carrie, who hadn't followed a word above the noise of the crowd and piped music, pretended to laugh.

"What's so funny? I said that's him over there, the one who fancies you."

"What…?"

"Over there. He's called Mick."

"Mick?" Carrie gaped. "That's Michael Deasy. He went to our junior school."

"What?" Annette couldn't hear because of the din, but what did it matter? Poor Michael Deasy, laughed at for years for his painful thinness and fishlike, short-sighted eyes was now blushing at her through steamed-up specs and a fresh crop of acne.

She could have cried she felt so sorry for him. Annette was yelling in her ear.

"Listen, lend us five quid, will you? We always put five each in the kitty and I'm broke."

After showing off about lending money to Katy she couldn't really say she had none. The notes came out of her pocket and Annette quickly grabbed at two of them.

"You said five," Carrie protested.

Annette waved the notes, "So? Five for me and five for you. Come on."

Two tables were being pushed together and they were all jostling for places.

Carrie took advantage of the confusion to make for the door, mumbling as she went, "I can't. I just remembered something and…" She was outside and nobody had heard a word. It was raining hard now and the street was busier, full of people going home from offices and factories, huddled under umbrellas or turned-up coat collars. Carrie pushed her cold hands deep into her pockets and began to run. The rain beat down on the top of her bare head. The pavements began to stream with water. She wasn't thinking of the black house now but of James, alone at the kitchen table with his mug of cocoa and his mouth tightly shut. She ran faster and harder until she just couldn't run any more and had to slow down to a walk.

"He's not on his own, he's not," she whispered, gasping for breath. "May wouldn't be late and leave him out in the rain, she wouldn't!" And breathless or not, she started running again, the rain streaming down her face like tears. Then she remembered again… "Mum's in! He's not on his own, Mum's in!" But the relief soon tightened into fear as she realised the trouble she would be in with her mum and she ran even faster, her soaked feet splashing through the puddles. There was a roll of thunder and the street lights went on.

She was crying as she sat on the bed drying her hair. She didn't make any noise but her shoulders shook and her eyes were squeezed tightly shut. Hot tears rolled down her cheeks and the cold rain rolled down the window in the darkened dreary world outside. She didn't want to cry aloud in case anybody came into her room. The worst thing was, though, that nobody would come in. Nobody wanted anything to do with her. Her mum was more upset than she was. She hadn't shouted or punished Carrie in any way. She had looked sick and frightened and as if she, too, might cry. It hadn't just been Carrie's lateness. That afternoon, Miss Swallow had telephoned to ask if Carrie was better, saying that three weeks' lessons seemed a lot to miss for even a very bad cold. By the time Carrie arrived home, an hour and a half late and soaking wet, her mother's anger and worry had turned to fear. She hadn't called the police but she had called the school and then Katy's house so she knew who Carrie had gone off with. That had not made her any less frightened. It had been awful. Even May, who always took the children's side when there was trouble, had looked at Carrie as though she didn't know her. She hadn't said anything except to whisper fiercely as Carrie passed her to leave the kitchen, "Your mammy was so scared when she didn't know where you were, she was sick, do you know that?" The lesson money had never been mentioned. Carrie had been sent to have a hot bath but now, even as she switched off the hairdryer and started plaiting her hair, she knew she couldn't possibly go down again. She was too upset to eat, but after sitting there in tears for a long time she expected somebody, even if it were only James, to come up and insist that she eat. Nobody did. She let herself cry louder but nobody heard, nobody came. Everybody hated her as much as she hated herself. On Friday nights, Dad always called from Hong Kong if he could, and she and James were allowed to stay up and talk to him. She heard the phone ring a couple of times but nobody called her. Nobody came. When Dad called, he would be told everything. Cold and miserable, she put on her thickest, snuggest pyjamas and crawled into bed.

"Katy," she sobbed, "I want to sleep at your house. I want your gran to put our hot water bottles in. I want somebody to talk to in the dark. Katy…"

But Katy had given her that same look which May had given her, as if she didn't know her any more. There was no Katy now, no hot water bottle, no friendly voice in the dark.

When, at last, she stopped crying because she was too weary to cry any more, she lay still, listening for noises from downstairs and wondering how she could face going down tomorrow morning. She decided the best thing to do would be to go straight to Gran's room and perhaps even have breakfast with her. Gran wouldn't look at her as if she didn't know her. Gran was always kind. She might not even know. Sometimes they didn't tell Gran unpleasant things because after her illness she mustn't be upset. Carrie would tell her and reassure her that it was all right, that she would never be so stupid again. This idea made her feel better, though her head hurt a lot, probably from crying. Now she was calmer she sat up and opened the tiny drawer of the velvety music box to make sure the silver locket and the key were still there.

"I'll show the music box to Gran tomorrow," she whispered to herself, "and Grandad's diary, too." She had a lot of things to tell Gran. Gran wouldn't hate her. She would help her to get the music box mended. She picked the box up now, opened the lid and shook it very gently, but the ballerina wouldn't come up or the music play. It was quite stuck. She left the box open and switched off her bedside lamp. She was shivering in spite of her thick pyjamas and her feet were icy. She tried to get warm by snuggling as far down under her quilt as possible. Soon she fell asleep.

When the music began at last, Katy rose up on her toes and began twirling slowly round. Then, still twirling, she seemed to float across the room hardly touching the floor with her points at all. How did she do that? She was a better dancer than anybody else in the class so perhaps that was the reason. The others weren't there, though. This wasn't the ballet school at all so they wouldn't be. Katy was dancing on a floor that was a mirror and the walls of the room were of pleated satin. That was the explanation. It was quite simple. This wasn't the ballet school.

"It's the music box," Carrie said aloud and opened her eyes in the dark.

It was the music box. Whatever had made it stick before, now it was going, the tiny ballerina twirling to the music, and it had woken her up. Carrie lay there with her head turned towards it, watching, but the ballerina's whirling made her aching head go round and she felt sick.

"It's too hot. I feel sick because it's too hot…" She sat up and pushed the quilt off her burning body. When she stood up her head and legs ached terribly.

"Got to get cool…" she mumbled. The attic, she decided, the attic was cold and the burning would stop. The music box had wound down so she closed its lid and picked it up. She went along the corridor to the attic stairs door without worrying about how very dark it was. All that mattered was that it was so hot. She felt in her box for the key and opened the door.

"That's better… cool…"

When she got up there she found that someone had left toys all over the bed. There was a drum and the Noah's ark and lots of other stuff. She pushed everything to the floor and climbed under the covers.

"My head hurts…" she said. Nobody heard. Nobody came. She fell asleep again.

The next time she opened her eyes she could just make out the shape of another bed and a chest of drawers, but they swayed about so much they made her feel seasick and she had to shut her eyes again. Outside in the night the rain fell steadily, pattering with cool fingers at the dark window. She wished the same cool fingers would touch her burning forehead but nobody came.

"Too hot…" She got up and tore off the suffocating thick pyjamas. Opening one of the drawers next to the bed she pushed the rolled-up pyjamas to the back of it and took out a cool starched cotton nightdress. As she pulled it on its scent of lavender soothed her aching head. She got back in bed and fell asleep at once.

"Edwina? Edwina! Will you get up out of that bed or will I come in there with a cold flannel?"

It was morning. The rain had stopped and the low sun shone in through the barred window, making a striped patch on the wallpaper. Speckles of dust turned slowly round and round in the sunbeam.

"Edwina!"

She sat up and swung her legs over the edge of the bed. For a moment she remained still, frowning. She had a feeling that something was peculiar but she couldn't think what. Was today her birthday or a special day of some sort? Had something important happened yesterday? She couldn't remember. She couldn't remember yesterday clearly at all.

"Edwina!"

That's what was odd. Her name… Her name was Edwina, of course, but today it sounded odd, as if she were hearing it for the first time, as if someone else were calling her by another name, someone calling her from farther and farther away until the sound faded and vanished. Then May appeared in her long apron with curling papers in her fringe and two big clean towels in her arms and everything went back to normal again.

"Will you get up out of that bed, Miss Edwina, or will I pull you out by the pigtail? If you want to wash in cold water it's all the same to me." The same speech she made every Saturday morning.

Edwina got up.

⤙ CHAPTER SIX ⤙

Edwina almost always lost her temper for one reason or another when she was getting dressed. The usual reason was that she knew she was going to be too hot all day but that nothing on earth would persuade May to let her leave off her flannel petticoat or her liberty bodice. As far as that was concerned May was just as bad as Nanny used to be, though, in every other way, she was a hundred times nicer. This morning it was different and Edwina had got into combinations, camisole, liberty bodice, knickers, flannel petticoat, cotton petticoat, socks, sailor blouse and navy blue pleated skirt without losing her temper a bit because she was so puzzled. The minute she had finished washing and was back in the night nursery, leaving May to the job of washing her struggling and protesting little brother, that funny feeling had come back. Now she sat on the bed with one boot on and the button hook in her hand, staring out of the barred window at the chimneys of the house opposite, trying her hardest to remember. To remember what? Well, of course, if she had been able to answer that question it would mean she hadn't forgotten, wouldn't it? It certainly wasn't her birthday and they weren't going on a journey or anything like that, but it was that sort of special feeling. The September morning was bright and fresh and the sky above the brown and black chimneys was a lovely pale blue but, nice as the day looked, it only meant a long dull walk with May or pulling little Jim around the back garden in the mail cart. Next door in the day nursery Jim was squealing.

"You're getting soap in my eyes! Let me go! Let me *go*!"

"Soap in your eyes, is it? Sure it's your ears as need the soap in them with the cabbages and potatoes sprouting in there in the dirt!"

Edwina pulled a face, remembering how much the hated smelly yellow soap stung and how May used to poke in her ears with the flannel. At least she was allowed to wash herself now that Nanny had gone and May had her hands full. She bent to insert the button hook and suddenly something flashed in her memory. Shoes… new shoes. She was sure she had been bought new shoes – and if she shut her eyes she could feel them, soft and comfortable like no shoes ever were. But the memory slipped away from her. She hobbled across the room in one sock and one flapping black boot to open the cupboard, but there were no new shoes there at all. It was just the same dreary line-up, all smelling of boot black except for her patent leather Sunday shoes, which looked so nice but hurt, and her bronze dancing slippers which she loved but hated, too, because they meant horrible dancing class this afternoon. She shut the cupboard and flopped into Nanny's old chair to poke the hook angrily into her boot, forgetting the strange feeling altogether and going back to her usual getting dressed temper.

"Will I help you with those, Miss Edwina?" May was at the door, her big apron all splashed from her struggles with Jim. Edwina held out her foot and

May came and took over the long boring job of buttoning.

"You're much faster than Nanny was," Edwina said, watching May's plump wrist turning. "May? I'm glad it was Nanny who went and you who stayed. I'm sure Mamma chose you because you're so much nicer."

"Are you now? Well, and I'm sure she chose me because I'm only a nursery maid and so much cheaper. Other foot. And when your little brother goes to school I wouldn't be surprised if I were to be sent packing, too, so there'll be nobody but Marjorie Weaks to button your boots for you, and how will you like that, Miss?"

"I shan't like it at all. I'm frightened of her funny eye."

"That's a walleye is what that is, not her fault at all, poor soul. An aunt of mine had a walleye."

"And did she die, May?" Edwina asked, hoping for a story.

"She did not. She married a man from Cork this very year though they all said she'd never catch a husband."

"Oh May, that's not a story!"

"Oh, isn't it? Well, my aunt thought it was, and a good one, too, and wasn't it her had the walleye, so she should know. Put on your pinafore now and go in there and sit up at the table for your porridge is cold as a fishmonger's slab."

Edwina hated porridge. She hated it even more than her flannel petticoat and her liberty bodice. It wasn't cold, though, but setting in its iron pan in the hearth. Edwina sat down at the table and glared at it as though she hoped a nasty enough look might make it disappear. The kettle for May's tea hissed and spat on the fire. The sunbeam from the window made the flames seem pale and gleamed on the grate which walleyed Marjorie Weaks polished with black lead every Saturday morning. Opposite Edwina, little Jim sat gripping his porridge spoon with a clean pink fist on the blue checked tablecloth, his red-gold hair wetted and combed and plastered down by May till it was quite stuck to his freckly forehead.

"Can I have a lot, May?"

"You can mind your manners, Master Jim, is what you can do," May answered sharply. She gave him a lot, even so. Jim was always hungry and Edwina usually managed to give him most of her porridge too. All she had to do was to sip at her milk and eat a few very tiny spoonfuls slowly while Jim gobbled and was told off for it. Then, usually while May was busy pouring her tea, she would swap her almost full bowl for Jim's almost empty one. She managed to do the swap just a few minutes later, putting a finger to her lips in warning. But poor little Jim who had suffered so many tellings-off from Nanny and then May about his manners, couldn't help himself.

"Thank you very—"

"Shh!"

Sometimes Edwina felt sure that May didn't notice things on purpose because she hated telling them off. She carried on pouring a stream of almost black tea into her flowered cup now without looking up and it wasn't long before Edwina was asking permission to leave the table and making for the door.

"You promised to play horse-and-cart with me!" protested Jim at once, still spooning up porridge.

"I'm going to see Mamma."

"Don't you go disturbing your mother, now, Miss Edwina," warned May, "and cod liver oil first, if you please."

"I'm not going to disturb her, I'm just going to say good morning to her." She gulped down the smelly oil and slipped from the sunny room to run along the cold corridor towards the staircase. It wasn't true that she was only going down to say good morning. There were two things she wanted, one usual and one special. When she tapped at her parents' bedroom door and no one answered, she knew she was in time for the first thing which was to find something good to eat. With a quick look over her shoulder to make sure that Marjorie Weaks wasn't coming up with her slops bucket, she opened the door and went in. Not so much sunshine came in through the muslin swags at the windows on this floor, but a bit of a fire was still burning in the grate so the room was pleasant and warm. The covers were thrown back over the foot of the high bed and the big white pillows were propped up and dented at the head. The room smelled of her mother's violet scented soap but though Edwina sniffed at the soap in its pretty porcelain dish, she was more interested in the morning tea tray. It was on the table by her mother's side of the bed. The teapot was cold and empty but there were three delicate fingers of bread and butter on the flowered plate. Three! This was treasure and Edwina ate them up quickly with an eye on the door. She took some pieces of sugar that remained in the bowl and left the bedroom, trying to suck the sugar and not crunch it so as to make it take the cod liver oil taste away and last all the way down the stairs. When she passed the dining-room door she heard Papa cough and Mamma say something to him that she couldn't catch. She didn't go in but went on and down the stairs to the kitchen, passing Marjorie Weaks coming up with her bucket.

"Don't you get in Cook's way this morning," Marjorie warned, "not with eight to dinner tonight."

Edwina ran on down the stairs, not answering and trying not to look at the eye. She didn't need to be told to avoid Cook who, whether there was a dinner party or not, was always in a bad temper because she didn't have a kitchen maid and had to make do with the bit of help Marjorie Weaks found time for between all her other duties. Luckily, she was outside now, giving the butcher's boy a good scolding for something or other, and Edwina was able to sneak through into the pantry without being seen. The cool pantry was a disappointment today. There was a big, half-eaten veal and ham pie on a plate, Papa's favourite but certainly not Edwina's. She hated meat. The big milk jugs, newly filled, stood with their round muslin covers over them. These covers had a crocheted edge with tiny coloured beads all around. One of the things Cook never understood was why Edwina was always asking for cups of milk. She was given plenty of milk up in the nursery so why come pestering down here? The reason was that Edwina just liked the beaded muslin covers and always took them off and put them back on herself if she could get Cook to let her. There seemed to be nothing at all to steal today. Of course you didn't often find anything worth eating down here. All the good things like the loaf sugar in its cones of thick blue paper and the tins of biscuits and the cocoa powder that you could dip your finger into and then lick were kept, like soap and candles, in the store cupboard to which only Mamma had the key. Even so, there was such a sweet fruity smell in the cool pantry that certainly had nothing to do with that great lump of a pie with its horrible jelly stuff on the thick pastry lid. Something much nicer, like when the jam was being made. Edwina soon found what it was. Cook had been stewing the big purple plums from the tree in the back garden and they were cooling in an earthenware bowl with a striped cloth over them. She lifted the cloth carefully and poked one finger into the red juice to pull out a plum, its yellow flesh bursting from the dark skin. It was as sweet and delicious as the jam they were given for Sunday tea, and she caught up the precious dribble of juice that rolled down her chin and sucked the last of it from her finger. Replacing the cloth, she came out of the pantry keeping a lookout for Cook. She was still out there shouting, thank goodness. On the big kitchen table Edwina saw the menu for tonight's dinner written in her mother's neat hand. She took a look at the list of good things.

Clear soup

Brill with shrimp sauce

Chicken patties
Roast pork with apple sauce
Roast potatoes
Cauliflowers in white sauce
Lettuce salad

Viennese pudding

Cheese straws
Cheese
Oranges, apples, raisins, walnuts

No such things were ever served in the nursery where the best you could hope for was usually boiled mutton and rice pudding.

Thomas, the kitchen cat, had taken advantage of the open door and the distracted Cook to sneak in and curl up to doze on a chair near the big black stove. He opened his eyes when Edwina appeared and she winked at him.

"I didn't spill anything today," she whispered. She always felt guilty when Thomas got blamed for the things she had stolen or knocked over but it couldn't be helped. Besides, he was a clever thief himself and much preferred a life of crime to the honest mouse catching which was supposed to be his job.

"Push the cat off that chair. I don't want him jumping up on the table."

The voice came into Edwina's head from nowhere. It was a voice she remembered, but whose voice? And the cat… it wasn't Thomas the voice was talking about but a fat grey cat. Thomas was black with a white bib. A grey cat and somebody nice… somebody… The memory melted away and Cook's voice came nearer and louder.

"I shall be round to that shop tomorrow myself and you can tell him so! And don't you give me any more of your cheek!"

Edwina ran out of the kitchen. Upstairs, she listened outside the dining-room door again and this time, instead of voices, she heard the chink of cups and saucers and cutlery. She knocked softly and went in. They didn't notice her at first, perhaps thinking she was Marjorie Weaks bringing more hot water for the teapot. She had timed it just right, as she almost always did. Papa, sitting with his back to the door was tapping at the top of his egg. Opposite him, Mamma sat behind the silver teapot reading a letter.

"But, Margaret, my dear…" Papa was saying, but he stopped and turned when he saw Mamma's rosebud lips break into a little smile.

"Ah, if it isn't my hungry little girl. Don't they give you anything to eat upstairs?"

"Porridge," said Edwina, pulling a face.

"But you do eat it up, dear, don't you?" Mamma asked with an anxious frown.

"Yes," Edwina lied. She was always being naughty but she couldn't bear to think of her mother knowing about it. "I'll tell your mammy about you, Miss," was the worst threat May could make. She opened her mouth to receive the top of Papa's egg. The best thing was that it was a hard boiled egg. The egg they were given upstairs for

Saturday tea was always soft boiled and Edwina hated the runny mess, especially if the white wasn't set enough. Edwina had a list of things she was going to have when she was grown up and could please herself. Hard boiled eggs were on the list and also white glazed kid boots instead of black leather ones, pale blue ribbon threaded through a white lace blouse like Mamma had on now, and never, ever, even when it snowed, flannel petticoats.

"Come and give me a kiss," Mamma said, holding out her pretty pink and white hand. Edwina went round to her and kissed her on the cheek that smelled of violets and was so soft above the rougher frills of her lace collar.

"Mamma…" Would she be allowed the second thing she was after? The special thing.

"Oh, Edwina," Mamma was pulling gently at her hair ribbon, "how can your hair be so tumbled about this early in the morning? I'm sure May brushed it nicely for you, didn't she? I'm afraid she has far too much to do since—"

"Margaret, please! Let's not go over that again. At least not in front of the child."

They were always saying "Not in front of the child" and it usually meant something they were quarrelling about. Edwina didn't want them quarrelling now. She wanted her mother's full attention and she wanted her in a good temper. And now they were talking and that was the worst thing of all because you couldn't interrupt. Edwina always chose breakfast time to try and get Mamma's attention because Papa always read his paper. He had finished his egg so why didn't he pick up the folded newspaper at his elbow instead of going on and on so that she couldn't speak to Mamma?

"Now the Ghost is finished there's nothing to delay the move to Derby and I'll have to make up my mind. Either way, we must retrench. The financial burden of setting up on my own would be much greater than that of a move, not to mention the question of the boy's school fees... Oh, we could stay, of course. I'm not saying the Old Man's wrong. Theoretically, my designs could be transmitted to a factory two hundred miles away — but seeing them become reality with my own eyes, watching every stage, correcting as we go along... It's my life's blood, Margaret..."

On and on he went and how Edwina longed to interrupt and ask questions. Not about the Ghost because she knew it wasn't a real ghost like May knew about, only a new car that Papa was forever talking about. He had even taken Jim to the works in Cook Street to see the engine. Edwina didn't care about that. It was the word "school" that made her heart beat louder. If *only* Papa would— He was, he was unfolding the paper and Mamma was reaching for the teapot. Would it be possible to get her attention before she opened another letter from the pile? The coals settled in the grate and the newspaper rustled, its warm pages smelling of fresh print. Papa struck a match and sucked at his pipe. Mamma's hand reached for a pale blue envelope. What could Edwina say that would be interesting enough to get her attention back?"

"Mamma?"

"Yes, dear?"

"Mamma, will I be beautiful like you when I'm grown up?"

"I expect so, dear." She picked up the letter knife.

"Mamma, May says if I go on tumbling my hair about and then crying when she has to comb the knots out, I shall have to keep it plaited all day."

"Did she? And will you like that?"

"No, I should hate it of all things!" Mamma was bored with her. She was opening her letter and once she started reading it, that would be interrupting. Desperate, Edwina blurted out her request. "Mamma, I want to go to school!"

"You've finished school, dear. You're much too big now to go to Miss Pargeter's. Besides, you read and write beautifully, though I'm afraid your French…"

"I mean a real school, Mamma, not Miss Pargeter's! All we ever did there was press flowers and do embroidery and read dull poems that she liked and we hated. I want to go to a real school. Caroline Emerson's going next week. And she has a uniform and she showed it to me when I went to tea after dancing class last Saturday. Please, Mamma, *please*.

"Caroline's father is a great scholar, Edwina, and has very particular ideas about things. We must try, later on, to find a mademoiselle to improve your French—"

"At home? Oh Mamma, please! If it's because they're richer than we are, there must be schools that cost less than the one Caroline's going to and I'll give up everything else. I'll… I'll not have a new dress again until I've finished school. There!"

"Edwina, please don't talk about money," Mamma said quietly. "Besides, you can't help growing out of your dresses, I'm afraid. Now, run along and play with your brother – and see that you do play with him, don't spend all morning stuffing indoors playing your flute. If May hasn't time to take you both for a walk you must get out in the garden. Promise?"

"Promise." She would promise anything to see her mother pleased with her but if May didn't drag them out for a walk she intended to play her flute for as long as she felt like.

"Off you go, then. Give your Papa a kiss and run along back upstairs."

"All right. But, Mamma, if I can't go to school can I at least have flute lessons instead of French?"

"I really don't think so, dear. Your French is very poor and you've had a year of flute lessons. Besides, you play to us very prettily as it is. And one day, when you're a grown-up married lady with children of your own you'll be able to play to your husband and your guests in the evenings and perhaps you'll even teach your own little girl to play."

"I should never have agreed to buy her the thing," Papa remarked without looking up from his paper. "Pianoforte should have been enough and have taken up less of her time."

"Nonsense, Edwin, you know you love to hear her play."

"Hmph."

Edwina thought her mother was very brave and wished she could sometimes say "Nonsense" to him like that. She went round to kiss him behind the newspaper. He had closed it and was reading the ads on the front page. She didn't like kissing him as much as Mamma. His soap was pleasant but not a really nice perfume like hers and the smell was mixed with pipe smoke. His cheek was almost as rough as his jacket. As usual, she sneaked a look at the concerts advertised in the paper.

BACKHAUS

ONLY
RECITAL
THIS
AUTUMN

SATURDAY
AFTERNOON NEXT
October 6th,
at 3 o'clock
will PLAY

Prelude C sharp minor ... ... Rachmaninoff
Impromptu, Op. 90, No. 4 ... ... Schubert

Edwina would have liked to hear that but something by a big orchestra would be even better because then there would be a flute there…

QUEEN'S HALL
PROMENADE CONCERTS

EVERY EVENING AT 8 O'CLOCK
THE QUEEN'S HALL ORCHESTRA

Conductor – Mr. Henry J. Wood
Solo violoncello – Mr. Jacques Renard
Solo flute – Mr. Albert Fransella

"Oh Papa, look!" Edwina gripped her Papa's arm. If only they lived in London. There weren't nearly so many concerts here, though once she had been taken to hear the Hallé Orchestra. But there was more to Edwina's "If only" than that. What she really longed for was to see in the paper:

Solo flute – Miss Edwina Grey

"Edwina, dear, run along now."

Edwina didn't move. A little cry escaped her lips which had turned white. Her grip tightened on Papa's arm as a feeling of panic welled up in her stomach and stopped her from breathing. In one brief flash, all the memories that had eluded her grasp this morning flooded into her head and, just for a moment, she remembered everything. Just for a moment she was Carrie, standing there in Gran's room where the furniture was just the same but there was no Gran, just two complete strangers.

"Mum…" That wasn't what she'd meant to say, and now she was falling, her cheek slipping down the rough sleeve she was holding.

"Edwina!"

"She's all right, Margaret. It'll be another of her tricks to avoid dancing class. Come on, now, old girl, pull yourself together."

She heard his voice but she could no longer see him. She felt herself spinning round and round in the dark and she slid down in spite of the arm trying to steady her.

Their voices came from far away.

"Oh Edwin, she's ill!"

"Damnedest thing, you'd think something she

spotted in the paper gave her a turn… I'll take her to the sofa in the drawing room."

The last thing Edwina felt before she lost consciousness altogether, was being carried in her father's arms through the draughty hall. The last thing she thought was that what he said was true. It was something she'd seen in the paper that had caused it. The date at the top of the page that was suddenly – though she didn't know why – wrong.

It said: SATURDAY, SEPTEMBER 29, 1906.

～CHAPTER SEVEN～

"SIT STILL."

"I am sitting still."

"Oh, are you? Well don't complain to me if I hurt you, that's all."

"Do you have to, May?"

"I must say, for one who wants to be a beauty like her mammy, you've little enough patience for it."

"Mamma doesn't have stupid sausage curls and, anyway, I'll never be as beautiful as she is."

Edwina had this same argument with May every Saturday afternoon when it came to getting ready for the hated dancing class. Jim hated it just as much as Edwina did but he never got into trouble over it, either because he was a boy or because he had a talent for ignoring what he didn't like rather than rebelling against it as Edwina did. They had both been stripped to the skin and scrubbed. Edward, half dressed, was playing with his precious model motor car under the table while Edwina sat on top with her back to the fire, having her dampened hair coiled into ringlets round May's plump finger. May called them sausage curls. Edwina hated those dreadful sausage curls almost as much as she hated porridge. They were frivolous, Caroline Emerson said. Caroline's hair was brushed straight and smooth, as became a serious girl who intended to be a writer when she grew up. It was impossible to imagine seeing a notice in *The Times* saying:

Solo flute... ... ...Edwina Grey

if the imaginary Edwina then walked onto the stage with sausage curls. Every time she tried it her dream collapsed into dreary reality at that point and her imaginary world dissolved to be replaced by black boots, liberty bodices, porridge and horse-and-cart in the sooty back garden.

"Glory be to God, will you give over wriggling like a serpent! It's the last of them I'm doing now."

There was some consolation in feeling her white organdie dress with its frilled yoke and blue silk sash pulled over her head. She loved the stiffness of the frills and the way it prickled under her arms – because she was growing, May said – and the huge shiny bow where the sash tied behind. It was almost as nice as Mamma's dresses and sometimes, on May's afternoon off, Edwina put it on all by herself and played the flute, pretending it was a concert.

"Will you wear your silver locket?"

That was nice, too. For her last birthday Mamma and Papa had given her a silver chain and a locket with their photographs in it, which she wasn't allowed to wear except on special occasions in case the chain got broken. Dancing class was considered special enough. There had once been an attempt to dress Jim in velvet knickerbockers for dancing class. He had submitted to this without a word but on the way there had, accidentally-on-purpose, slipped and fallen into a deep puddle much tainted with horse dung and had had to be brought back home. The experiment was not repeated and he was now fastened into his usual tweed knickerbockers and Norfolk jacket.

Edwina hurried into the night nursery where her blue velvet jewellery case sat on the chest of drawers by her bed. She loved that jewellery case, though she had nothing other than her silver locket to put in it. She loved it because it was a music box and she wound it up very carefully now. Her father had warned her last Christmas morning that it must be wound slowly and carefully and never too much or, like a watch, the spring would break. She set it down and opened the lid. The music began to play and, like magic, a delicate porcelain ballerina rose up and twirled about on a satin-covered pedestal above a round mirror, which reflected her lacy white ballet dress tinged with pink. It was the prettiest thing Edwina had ever owned and, although it was real, for her it was part of her perfect dream world in which she played solo flute and her little ballerina danced and the audience applauded them both. The ballerina didn't have stupid sausage curls. Her dark hair was drawn tightly back, her tiny face pure white and her lips red.

"I wish I didn't have to go out," Edwina whispered to her. With the excuse of having fainted she had been allowed to stay indoors all morning and had almost, but not quite, learnt to play the music box tune on her flute. "Tomorrow, after church, if—"

"Hats and coats, now," shouted May, interrupting. Crossly, Edwina closed her music box and came to be buttoned into her good fawn coat with the cape and fur collar.

"I'll be too hot, May!"

"I'll be the judge of that." May looked hard into Edwina's face. "Are you all right?"

"I suppose so," Edwina admitted reluctantly. The trouble was that she couldn't remember at all what had happened before she had wakened on the drawing-room sofa by the fire and found three worried faces staring into hers.

"She must be ill," Mamma had said.

"Too much stuffing indoors with that flute," Papa had said.

"Another dancing class trick," May had said, and her word had been final so that now there was no escape.

"Now, have I your shawls and your fancy shoes?"

All the way along the cool and sunny streets Edwina tried her hardest to remember what had made her faint like that but she couldn't. Twice they saw a motor car and had to stop for Jim to look at it. Only once, thank goodness, did they see a poor starved horse beaten until he bled, when he couldn't pull his load of coal and kept falling down as his legs buckled under him. They almost had to run, May covering Edwina's eyes to stop her crying, though she still did.

As usual, they had to cross the street and walk on the other side so as not to pass close by the legless beggar who always sat at the entrance to a dark alley between two houses. Edwina was terrified of him and was sure he would grab at her with a bony hand if she went near him. May said this was nonsense but they crossed over anyway.

"For I've nothing to give him and besides, these beggars are up to all sorts of tricks. If you ask me, he's sitting on his legs, got them tucked away under him. Get a move on now, or it's half an hour late you'll be."

And then the hated dancing class was underway.

"And skip and two and three and four and skip and two and three, four!" Thank goodness there were only two boys in the class, apart from Jim, who had already been sent out of the room for racing during the polka – he was convinced that the way to "win" at dancing was to get to the end of it before the music did – so Edwina could dance with Caroline whose straight hair and simple, sashless frock made her feel ridiculous herself, but proud of her intellectual friend.

"And round and two and three, four and round and two and three, four!" bellowed Miss Pendleton, her fat brown frilly chest heaving up and down in time to the music of the barn dance.

Edwina thudded round with Caroline, trying to keep her nostrils closed against the musty dancing-class smell which came, she thought, partly from the unwashed wooden floorboards, partly from the dark blue cloth covering the back of the upright pianoforte and partly, or perhaps mostly, from Miss Deasy, the pianist, whose rigid back suggested corsets as tight as her thin lips and whose hat was loaded with dusty violets and wax cherries, bobbing as she played.

"And march into line… and… point – left toe, Celia, *left*!"

As the girls swept their pointed left toes behind them, holding out their skirts in a final curtsey, and the boys bowed, Celia Lofthouse fell over, lost her round spectacles and started howling, as she did almost every week.

"And who can blame the child?" May said under her breath as she pulled at the crossed elastic and whipped off Edwina's bronze slippers. "The size of her! Dressed up in all them frills like an elephant at the circus!" Poor Celia was still sobbing as her nurse buttoned her coat for her.

"Can we go to the circus, May?" asked Jim.

"To see a lot of wicked little monkeys that's as bad as yourself, do you mean?"

"No, May, to see the elephants in frills. Can we?"

"You can hold them shawls over your ears and mouths is what you can do or you'll catch your deaths and have me up all night with your coughs and your earaches. And straighten that cap."

"It won't be cold, May!"

The shawls were big and cumbersome and made of itchy mohair and when you held them over your mouth your breath made wet drops collect in them so that they itched even more. It wasn't very cold but cooler than before now the sun was going down. The hoot of a motor car's horn set Jim tugging at May's hand to get to the edge of the pavement, but with a clatter of hoofs and rattling wheels, a horse tram, thundering towards town, blocked his view.

"It's gone, May! Why didn't you let me go? Now it's gone!"

"Nasty, smelly objects, motor cars are," May said.

"You wouldn't dare say that if my Papa were here."

"That's true but he's not and they make a terrible stink and a row, so they do."

"You don't know anything about it because you haven't been in one and I have. May! Conkers, May!" Jim tore free of May's restraining hand and ran forward.

"Don't you dare pick up things from the street, that's common!"

"Do let him, May," Edwina begged. Her little brother was a pest but at least conkers were a change from his everlasting motor cars and the shiny brown treasure hidden among the big golden leaves all along the avenue made her wish she were a boy and could hunt them for herself. Perhaps May felt the same way. In any case, once she'd made her protest she slowed her walk through the thick carpet of leaves and began telling Edwina about a conker her brother had kept for three years.

"Nobody had one that could beat it and in the end it was stolen from him. Ah, he was a great one to soak a conker in vinegar and bring it out so hard it could kill a man."

"And did it kill a man, May?"

"It did not, for Michael-Joseph wouldn't harm a fly – what's the matter with you?"

"I… I don't know… May!"

"What is it? You look as if you've seen a ghost. There's nothing but a field there."

What May said was true. They had left the avenue behind and there were no houses here, only a small churned-up field where a few tradesmen's horses searched half-heartedly for something edible among the soot-blackened weeds. Edwina hadn't seen a ghost exactly. Voices… there were voices all around her, calling and laughing. One voice called, "Carrie!" from behind her and she whipped round as though someone had called her name. The street was empty except for a boy carrying a tray of meat on his head. The boy's lips were puckered as though he were whistling but Edwina couldn't hear him whistle because of the voices, hundreds of them now, and a bell ringing, not like a church bell but like an alarm bell, on and on, louder and louder. Edwina put her hands over her ears but May was holding them, trying to pull them away. She was shouting something but the voices drowned her words.

"Carrie! Carrie! Carrie!" There were people everywhere and, just for a split second, a building, a large red brick building. Then the field, the grazing horses, and silence.

"Dear God, child, what's happened to you? You're as white as a sheet. Was it a vision you saw? Saint Theresa? An angel?"

"No. I… it was voices. I heard a lot of voices." May made the sign of the cross on herself. "And I saw a big building. Did there used to be a big building here once, May? I don't mean in the olden days, I mean when I was very small."

"A building? I never heard of anyone having a vision of a building. Were there pearly gates at the front of it at all? Golden towers? A big light shining from it, anything of that sort?"

"No, it was a red brick building with big windows. I must have seen it before because I remembered it. I even knew what was inside it. It was a school, a real school like Caroline Emerson's going to—"

"Ah, so that's it, and me thinking you were chosen. This is all hysterics because you want to go to school and your parents can't afford it."

"How do you know they can't afford it?"

"I know a great many things."

"Well, it's not true – I mean it's not true that it's hysterics. I did see a building, honestly I did."

But May ignored her. She was calling to Jim who had reached the next corner and then turned back to come running towards them, his pockets bulging with conkers and his cheeks red with excitement.

"Will you stop that running! You'll fall!"

"May! Come quick, May!" He didn't fall but he skidded into May's open arms, almost knocking her over. "The hurdy gurdy man's there, May! Edwina! The hurdy gurdy man!" He took the hand of each one and dragged them on to the corner of a cobbled street. There, a group of ragged little boys, with broken boots and no socks, were taking turns to throw stones at the hurdy gurdy man, who was too far down the street and surrounded by little girls for them to hit him.

"Don't you dare go near them common boys, now," warned May, hauling Jim back as he tried to make a dash for freedom and the stone-throwing boys. Jim, frustrated, threw a conker half-heartedly in their direction.

Edwina placed herself almost behind May and peeped out. She was frightened, not just of the hurdy gurdy man with his long white beard and dusty clothes, but of the hurdy gurdy itself, a black and nasty-looking contraption strapped to the man's neck and propped up by one thin wooden leg. And yet she was fascinated by the music he was churning from it. Fascinated and astonished.

"May, listen, it's my tune, my music box tune. How does he know it, May? Why is he playing it?"

"It's a free country. Jim, don't you dare move or we go home directly!"

Round and round went the tune, just like the music box, while the little girls from all the poky houses in the street danced solemnly. They didn't dance with each other, but each one alone. They didn't laugh and skip and their faces wore an expression of great concentration as they held their pinafores out primly and their dirty boots followed the rhythm with great precision. The low September sun sent out long rays from behind the spire of St Paul's Church to light the scene from behind. The ragged boys were snaking forward close to the houses to where they might get a better aim. A woman opened her door, perhaps to call one of the little girls in and the hurdy gurdy man stretched his free arm towards her, holding out a battered hat for money. Then Edwina noticed one special girl. She was noticeable because she wasn't holding her pinafore out like all the others but dancing with her arms, waving them gracefully above her head. She was special because of that and because her dark hair was drawn tightly back from her delicate white face and her pretty lips were red.

"She's my ballerina…" Fascinated, Edwina forgot her fear of the hurdy gurdy man and ran forward into the group of dancing children.

"Miss Edwina!" But May was too late and too occupied with holding the struggling Jim to catch her.

The girls were annoyed but, seeing Edwina's shining curls and rich clothes, they moved aside one by one and let her through. As she came close, a ray of low sunlight touched the girl's dark hair and Edwina stopped dead.

"Katy…?" she said softly, without knowing why. Then the last of the girls blocking her way moved aside and she saw. Saw why the child was dancing with her arms, saw why she stayed in the same spot while the others moved around her, saw the twisted little legs propped up by ugly black iron splints. Then the sunbeam was in her eyes, blinding her and she covered her face with her arm, screaming.

"Katy! No! Oh no!" She turned and ran, and above the din of the hurdy gurdy she heard the children laughing at her. A sharp stone hit her between the shoulder blades and she ran faster towards May and safety, still screaming as though her heart would break.

━ CHAPTER EIGHT ━

THEY RAN ALL the way home. Edwina still crying, hardly feeling her feet touching the ground. May ran her hardest to get Edwina away, knowing she would be in trouble for letting her get into hysterics again. Jim just enjoyed the excitement and the running. Every so often a chestnut spilled from his bulging pockets and he would drag on May's arm to try and stop for it.

"Stop that! Run! Come on, run!" And they ran.

It wasn't until much later, with all the

explanations, excuses and admonitions over and high tea in the nursery eaten, that things really calmed down. Edwina, warm and sleepy after all that crying, was curled up in the battered brown armchair in front of the nursery fire, which was fed to a cheerful blaze for May's ironing. Jim was on his Scots Greys rocking horse, making subdued trumpet and drum sounds and giving muffled orders as he charged the French infantry squares at Waterloo. Anything noisier and he'd have had May to battle with, never mind Napoleon. Edwina, her sore eyes closed, listened to the swish and clatter of the iron and Jim's murmurings. She felt exhausted but very relaxed. She wished she could stay here just like this all night. It was so cosy by the fire and the room smelled of buttered toast and ironing. But when she peeped through half-closed eyes she saw May flicking water on the last starched cotton petticoat and soon the iron clanged down on its stand.

"Seven o'clock. Bedtime. Come on, now!"

"Oh May!" they both wailed at once.

"I'm still hungry, May!" said Jim.

"Hungry, is it? And you with enough buttered toast inside you to feed all of Wellington's army. Not to mention Edwina's egg as well as your own.

If you'd fill your stomach, Miss, instead of filling your head with nonsense about poor people who are probably no better than they should be, we'd have less hysterics."

"Oh May, I couldn't eat it. The white was all slimy. It always is when Marjorie Weaks boils our eggs. Why can't Cook do it?"

"That's right. Why can't Cook do it? Isn't it she who has nothing else to do with only eight to dinner tonight? And if I'm not down there helping in five minutes there'll be murder committed, so get to your beds. And no story, so don't ask me. I've my fancy outfit to put on."

If Jim and Edwina scrambled into their pyjamas and into their beds without any more "Oh-Maying" it was because they had every intention of getting up again almost as soon as she'd gone downstairs. They loved it when May acted as parlour maid. She always pretended not to see them on the stairs but, as soon as she thought it was safe, she would come up to tell them off and send them back to bed with a napkin full of delicious dinner party food. Their mother refused to have a maid in from outside, convinced that she would let robbers into the house while they were all at dinner, and May was always glad enough of a few shillings extra to send home to her mother for her numerous hungry brothers and sisters.

They snuggled down now with the blankets up to their chins, pretending to be asleep while May got changed into her maid's uniform over by her bed, managing to do it by the faint glow of Jim's night-light. May always said she didn't mind a bit sharing their room. At home she had shared a big bed with three sisters and besides, she said, it was better than "that cupboard of a place off the kitchen with its fold-away bed" where poor Marjorie Weaks spent her nights and kept her few belongings.

Peeping out, Edwina saw May reach behind her to unfasten the big safety pin that fastened her long blue skirt to her white flannel blouse. It always amazed Edwina how many hot uncomfortable clothes May wore, even though she was practically a grown-up and there was no one to force her into them. Once, watching secretly when May went to bed, Edwina had actually counted fourteen pieces, if she counted both boots and both black woollen stockings. Apart from those and the blouse and skirt, she counted a high starched white collar, fastened with studs, a long flannel petticoat, a short flannel petticoat, a white cotton petticoat bodice with buttons and tapes, white cotton drawers with buttons and tapes, horrible bony grey stays with suspenders, white cotton combinations with plenty of buttons and tapes and thick, long-legged, long-sleeved, scratchy woollen combinations.

Edwina had said to her next day, "When I'm grown up I shall leave off all my petticoats." May had answered, "Indeed, you'll do no such thing for it wouldn't be respectable." Why petticoats made you respectable she was unable to explain to Edwina's satisfaction and so leaving off petticoats remained on her list of things to do when grown up. In the meantime, the respectable May had no idea that Edwina watched her buttonings and unbuttonings and would have been very shocked had she discovered it. She was putting on a long black frock now and over that a white apron and a frilly white mobcap. Then she folded her own clothes, put them away in her drawer and went out, shutting the door softly.

"Jim," Edwina whispered, "are you awake?"

"Of course I am. We're going down, aren't we?"

"We have to wait at least half an hour. I haven't heard the door knocker yet and May's only just gone down."

"All right."

To help pass the time Edwina sat up and wound up her music box but as soon as the ballerina began turning she wished she hadn't done it. The tiny white face and dark, tightly-drawn hair reminded her of the poor dancing girl with ugly irons on her legs and at once she felt her own face grow tight and hot and tears fill her eyes again. Infantile paralysis. Mamma had said that was almost certainly what was wrong with the girl but May knew better and said it was rickets. "For her legs was very crooked and that's a fact. The irons, now, they'd be to make them grow straighter." Mamma had used the opportunity to warn Edwina that this was what happened to children who got too little food and fresh air, and a great deal was said on the subject of porridge and cod liver oil and playing outside rather than playing the flute. Luckily, the whole thing was kept from Papa so that May was saved a scolding for the episode and, at the end of it all, kind Mamma gave Edwina a florin to put in the collection box for crippled children. Back in the nursery, Edwina had hoped for something more about rickets. Surely one relation of May's or another must have had it. But May had answered tartly, "Indeed they did not. No child in our family ever went short of milk and fresh air and my own mother has brought up nine. That sort of thing goes on in towns, not in the country."

"But she has no mother, May!"

"And how would you know?"

"I don't know how I know. I just know…" And she had called her Katy without knowing why that should be, either. All she knew for sure was that this time she couldn't and wouldn't run away from something that made her cry. She had to find a way to help that girl. She leaned back against her propped-up pillow and, as the ballerina turned more and more slowly and the music wound down, she made a plan.

"Edwina! Edwina! It's much more than half an hour – it must be two hours at least!"

"No it isn't. Put your dressing gown on and keep your voice down."

There wasn't really any need to whisper since no one downstairs could possibly hear what was going on up in the attic. They were whispering because they were doing something naughty. And once their dressing gowns were tied over their nightgowns they did something much naughtier, something which, if anyone were to find out, would mean a spanking.

The trouble was that Jim was so terrified of the

ghosts he said came out of the stained-glass window on the first landing, that he refused to go down with only a bedside candle. Candlelight, he said, wasn't enough to discourage a ghost from showing itself and, besides, candlelight flickered and made giant shadows that moved by themselves on the wall and could grab at you just as easily as the coloured ghosts from the stained glass. What you needed against ghosts was bright blue-white gaslight but that was only in the rooms downstairs. The grown-ups weren't scared of ghosts because they went along the corridors and up and down the stairs with oil lamps. Now, oil lamps being dangerous things, children weren't allowed to touch them and were left to fight off ghosts with a feeble little candle, which wasn't fair at all.

Edwina lit Jim's bedside candle from the nightlight and gave the candlestick to him to carry. In bare feet, they crept through the day nursery and out into the corridor where the oil lamps used by May on the attic stairs, stood in a line on a small table outside the door. There Edwina, who always watched grown-ups carefully and knew how things were done, lifted the glass globe from a lamp and turned up the soaked wick enough for it to be lighted from Jim's candle. She replaced the globe and the light burned brightly, protected from the cold draughts in the corridor and stairs. Then she stuck the candle back into Jim's candlestick for him and whispered fiercely, "You carry that carefully and keep it away from my hair — and don't you ever dare tell about the oil lamp, not even to May or I'll murder you with Cook's biggest knife *and* I'll never take you down when there's a dinner party again!"

"I won't tell, Edwina."

And they began their journey down. It took a long time because they had to pass some very difficult places that required special manoeuvres. For instance, there was one stair on the attic staircase that creaked loudly and was so frightening in the silence that it made you jump and you ran the risk of dropping your lamp or candle. So the best thing was to sit down on the stair above the creaky one and place your feet on the one below it, then get up again. Jim had to be convinced to wait until Edwina was standing again before he sat down on the stair because that was where he had once singed her hair with his candle. The smell of singed hair is very strong and lasts for hours. May had smelled it when she came up to bed and her relentless questioning had got some of the truth out of Jim and got them both a spanking.

"What sense is there, anyway, in the person behind carrying a light? If you'd any sense you'd have the person in front hold it!" She never found out about the oil lamp.

The next danger to be faced after the creaking stair was the tall black narrow cupboard on the corridor near their parents' bedroom. This cupboard was a worry even in the daytime. The corridor was always gloomy and the thing looked so much like an upright coffin that if its door creaked open there would surely be a dead body inside which, being upright, could easily fall on you. This thought was even more dreadful in the deathly silence of the night and, though she never would admit it, it frightened Edwina just as much as Jim. On the landing below stood the grandfather clock inside which — Jim swore he'd seen her — lived a ragged old woman with bony legs whose job it was to pull on the brass pendulum to make the huge mechanism tick and tock and sound the hours. Obviously, she was starving since there was no food in there. Jim said she was on good terms with Marjorie Weaks and that she was the one who ate the leftovers of bread and butter and sugar from the breakfast tray which Cook accused Marjorie Weaks of taking. Edwina knew better about the leftovers but the image of the bony-legged woman was a frightening one when you passed by the tall, loudly ticking clock. Next they had to pass the stained-glass window which Jim managed by holding on to Edwina's dressing gown and keeping his eyes fixed firmly on the bright oil lamp. At last, with the lamp turned off and safely camouflaged among all the others on the table at the bottom, they settled to wait on the lowest staircase.

"I told you we'd waited too long," whispered Jim. Noises of cutlery and conversation coming from the dining room on the left meant that the dinner was underway and they had missed the procession of couples crossing the hall from the drawing room. They always enjoyed spotting their friends' parents and Edwina liked to look at the ladies' evening dresses, especially if there happened to be a new bride wearing her wedding dress. Still, they managed to sneak down between the serving of courses and warm their cold feet at the remains of the drawing-room fire and be back on the stairs in time for May to chase them away at the end of dinner, thrusting into Edwina's hands a huge napkin filled with food. It was a good haul tonight. Sitting on their cold beds, the oil lamp safely extinguished, they shared out the food by candlelight. There was a chicken patty each, a stick of celery to be measured and divided with Jim's pocket knife, some raisins and slices of apple and four cheese straws. By the time the sharing-out was completed, Jim had eaten most of his.

"Don't you want yours?" he mumbled through a mouthful of cheese straw.

"Yes, I do," Edwina said, but she didn't eat anything. She wrapped her food up in the napkin again and hid it in the corner of the top drawer of the chest by the bed. That was part of her plan. Whether she would be able to carry it out or not depended on May and a certain policeman.

"Jim? Can you remember if… Jim?"

But Jim, his stomach for once filled to his satisfaction, was already fast asleep.

Sunday afternoon in the park, according to Jim, was rotten compared to other afternoons. The first reason was that they were dressed in their best clothes which were uncomfortable and hadn't to be got dirty. The second reason was that, being in their best clothes, they had to walk there instead of going in the mail cart. Edwina didn't mind so much because her everyday clothes were just as uncomfortable as her Sunday ones, without looking so nice and because, being so much bigger, she always had to be the horse pulling between the shafts while Jim rode in the cart and rattled at the reins harnessed to her chest. Besides, there was more going on in the park on Sundays. There was always a band playing if the weather was fine, and red, white and blue bunting fluttering around the bandstand. Often there was a balloon man who sold monkeys that climbed sticks, too, and there was always an ice-cream cart with a bell. Most of their pocket money got used up in the park, but today Edwina had other plans for the sixpence and the threepenny bit tucked into her pinafore pocket together with Mamma's florin. The pocket was filled to bursting point because, after the money, she had stuffed it with last night's food from the dinner party, plus a bit of bread and butter and some pieces of sugar taken from Mamma's tea tray this morning. Jim's pockets bulged with conkers, some of which were strung ready for battle, and May was carrying a bag of stale crusts of bread for them to feed to the swans on the lake.

An old woman held out flowers to them as they passed and Edwina tried to get May to let her stop and look at them.

"Come away! I can smell the gin on her breath from here."

"I can smell Papa when he drinks some whisky," Jim declared, "and when I grow up I'm going to drink a whole bottle of whisky myself."

"Then you'd better not grow up at all," said May.

"The band's playing, May!" Edwina cried. "Listen!" They had reached the gates.

"I'm not sitting near the bandstand, May! There's nobody to play with if we sit there, there's just boring grown-ups. May, if your policeman comes will you ask him if I can try his helmet on just for one minute?"

"I will not."

"Why won't you, May, if he's your friend?"

"And who told you he's my friend, Master Jim Grey?"

"Edwina said."

"Be quiet, Jim! If you get May in trouble…"

"I haven't *done* anything, have I, May? Edwina's always telling me off when I haven't done anything. May, look! There's Charles Emerson and he's got a conker!" May grabbed at his hand just in time to stop him dashing away.

"Come back here! And where's your glove?"

"Lost it. I've got the other one."

"And what use is one glove, I'd like to know? Give it to me." May had a collection of Jim's odd gloves for which the other never turned up. And since she daren't tell Mamma too often that yet another pair had to be bought, Jim managed to go without the hated gloves for most of the time which Edwina thought was very clever of him. He was dragged along protesting until they reached their usual bench but little Charles had seen Jim, too, and the Emersons' nurse was being pulled along to join them. The Emersons' nurse wore a grey uniform and a hat with streamers and the first time they'd all met in the park, she hadn't wanted to speak to May who was only a nursery maid and had no uniform. But Caroline and Charles had insisted on playing with Edwina and Jim and, in the end, the pleasure of gossiping overcame the rules of snobbery.

"What a beautiful afternoon it is," said the large uniformed nurse as they arrived. "Well, Miss Edwina, you'll have no playmate today. Miss Caroline is reading an essay she's written to her father. I don't hold with all this staying indoors myself, I must say."

"Quite right, too," agreed May. "Will you sit a while?"

They were soon deep in talk, all the interesting bits being whispered. Edwina usually liked to sit very quietly with her head turned towards the bandstand as though she were attending to the music. Sooner or later they would forget all about her and she would strain her ears to catch some of those fascinating whisperings. Today, though, she wished the Emersons' nurse would go away. Her plan depended on May's policeman and he would never dare approach if May wasn't alone.

"So I said to her, I said, Madam, I said, that's as may be but in that case I must give notice."

"You didn't! I'd never have dared say such a thing at all."

"Well not in so many words, of course, but I *did* say…"

On and on, whisper, whisper, whisper. Oh why didn't she go?

May was perhaps thinking the same thing because, although she was keeping up with the conversation, her eyes were straying left and right, left and right, watching the people strolling by under the golden trees. She was looking out for him, Edwina was sure, and sometimes she sneaked a look at the watch pinned to Caroline's nurse's grey cloak. Even so, the band had played four more tunes before the fat nurse got up to go.

"There's that filthy ice-cream cart coming. I

don't want him asking for ice cream or there'll be
no end to it. Full of germs, that stuff is, I'm sure.

Poor little Charles was hauled away in the
middle of a conker game and Jim ran up shouting,
"May, the ice-cream man!"

"It's full of germs, her ladyship says, did you
know that? I think I shall have one myself. Sit
down here, now, and be good until he gets here. Do
you hear his bell?"

But it wasn't the ice-cream man's bell that made
May so excited that her cheeks turned pink and
her eyes sparkled. Edwina couldn't see the
policeman but May must have spotted him in the
crowd and he couldn't be far away. She had to
move fast.

"May, I don't want any ice-cream. Can I go and
feed the swans?"

"All right, but stay on this side of the lake where
I can see you and don't lean over the railings." May
said the same things she always said, but she wasn't
even looking at Edwina as she handed over the bag
of crusts.

"Afternoon, Miss May."

There he was! Edwina prodded Jim, held a
finger to her lips and frowned to remind him of all
the terrible things she would do to him if he told.

She walked across the fresh-smelling grass to the low railing at the edge of the lake and stood there with the paper bag in her hand, glancing over her shoulder every minute or so until she was sure that May and her policeman were absorbed in conversation. The swan who had sailed towards her expecting to be fed, rose in the water and made a little flurry with his wings. Then he settled there and waited. A sparrow hopped along the grassy edge, chirrupping, in the hope that a few crumbs might come his way.

With a last furtive glance behind her, Edwina stuffed the bag of crusts in her coat pocket and ran away.

—CHAPTER NINE—

EDWINA HAD NEVER in her whole life been out in the street alone. It was so exciting that, once outside the park gates, among so many people and noisy carriages, she was afraid that in her agitation she would get lost, although she knew well enough which way to take. She had to go back towards home first and then go the way they went every week to walk to dancing class. The strange thing was that without May and Jim beside her it looked quite different and she noticed things she had never noticed before. She could go slowly and look up at the blue sky above the chimneys. She could also stop and look at things whenever she felt like it instead of being hurried along. It was some time before she realised this and at first she rushed along as though being pulled, hardly glancing at the fine carriages rattling along on the cobbles and the many strolling couples out for a Sunday turn in the glowing autumn sunshine. It was a voice that first stopped her.

"Buy a few nice flowers, Miss?" It was the old woman selling her tiny bunches of flowers to the ladies and gentlemen on their way to and from the park. Edwina stopped and looked at her, trying to decide if she really smelled of gin. Her old face was creased and whiskers sprouted on her chin. She wore an old-fashioned bonnet with one of her own posies pinned on it for decoration. In spring she sold violets and primroses for the ladies and there were always roses or carnations for gentlemen's buttonholes. Today her basket was filled with roses and their perfume was strong in the fresh sunny air. Edwina didn't know what gin smelled like but she was sure that May had been wrong. Edwina loved flowers but she especially loved perfumed flowers like these. Sometimes she sniffed at the ones in the little silver vases in Mamma's bedroom or on the small tables in the drawing room but she had never held a bunch of her own. The dusty Canterbury bells and cornflowers growing beside the path to the front door in the shade of soot-blackened laurels were too sad and ugly to be worth picking.

"Sixpence for a nice little posy, Miss. Take one." A grimy hand held out the sweet pink buds. Nobody told Edwina to come away at once. In her pinafore pocket nestled a florin, a sixpence and a threepenny bit. She was free to do as she wanted. As if hypnotised, she fished out her sixpence and another grimy hand shot forward like lightning and grasped it. It was gone. The flowers were thrust into her hand but the old woman's hand didn't quite let them go.

"I've seen you before, Miss, haven't I?"

"Yes," answered Edwina in a whisper. Did she know that Edwina had run away from May? Was she going to shout for May's policeman?

"I thought as much. I've seen you with your little brother and you look at my basket of flowers like you'd eat them for two pins."

"It's the perfume I like," said Edwina more loudly and bravely now. "I don't want to eat them at all."

"Of course you don't. No offence, little lady. It was just a manner of speaking. You're a proper little beauty, too. You'll see when you grow up how the young men'll be sending you flowers."

"They will not," Edwina told her, "because I don't want a young man. I'm going to be a musician and play the flute in an orchestra and people will give me huge bunches of flowers at the end of my concerts."

"Is that right?" the old woman said, staring at Edwina in surprise. "Well, a fine young lady like you's going to want a husband, even so."

"I shan't want one at all," said Edwina firmly. "Thank you very much for the flowers. Good afternoon."

She thought she had dealt with that very well but then she heard the old woman chuckling as she walked away her face went hot and red and thought that perhaps she had sounded ridiculous. She had wanted to sound serious like Caroline Emerson but Caroline would never have spent her money on flowers. How stupid she had been! Only then did she remember in a rush of dismay that all her money had been meant for the poor crippled girl. She ran away, clutching the spray of flowers in her gloved hand, almost in tears.

"How could I have done it? How wicked and selfish I am!" She ran until she was out of breath and then slowed down, thinking what to do. It was quite simple. She would give the pretty flowers to the poor girl. How she would love them, living in that dirty little street without so much as a scrap of garden. No grown-up contradicted her. No one took the flowers from her and told her to stop her foolishness. She walked on down the sunny street, happy and excited again. Then she remembered that she couldn't hope to get away with more than a very brief absence, no matter how much in love May might be, and she walked faster. As she rushed along, she imagined the scene which would soon take place as she gave the crippled girl the flowers, money and nice things to eat. It was such a touching scene, like something out of a story book, that it almost made her cry. So it was that, distracted by her dream, her vision blurred with welling tears, she forgot to cross over in the usual place. He grabbed at her arm with a hand like a claw. Edwina screamed but none of the strolling ladies and gentlemen heard her above the clatter of hooves and wheels. She tried to yank her arm away but the bony grip closed tighter.

"Just a few coppers, Miss. You look to me like you can spare them. All by yourself today, are you?"

"I am not! I'm not by myself, my nurse is coming and if you don't let me go she'll tell a policeman!" Edwina's heart was thumping fit to burst, she was so frightened.

"You're by yourself. I saw you coming along. All I want is a few coppers, Miss. What can a man without legs do except beg? I was respectable once."

In spite of her fear which was calming down now that the man was speaking to her just like an ordinary person, Edwina couldn't help being curious. May had told a lie, anyway because the beggar was certainly not sitting with his legs under him. The stumps bound with dirty rags were real.

"I'll give you threepence," Edwina promised, "if you'll let me go."

"You won't run away?"

"No, I promise." The filthy hand relaxed its grip and Edwina pulled open her coat and fished out the threepenny bit from her pocket. The beggar grabbed it and it vanished into some hidden pocket of his own.

"That's a nice warm coat you've got," he said as Edwina refastened it. Did he want to steal it? It wouldn't fit him… but what if he had a little girl? A little girl like Katy, perhaps with no legs at all like him.

"What happened to your legs?" she asked him. "Was it rickets?"

The beggar laughed. "No," he said, "it was the Boers."

"What's that? Is it an illness?"

"Not an illness. A war."

"Did you fight Napoleon?"

He laughed again. "Do I look like I'm a hundred?"

Edwina blushed at her ignorance. The little history and geography Miss Pargeter had offered between poetry and pressing flowers, hadn't prepared her for this conversation but the beggar wasn't angry, at least.

"No… you don't look quite a hundred…" His tangled hair and beard were certainly not white like a very old man's. It was hard to tell what colour they were because they just looked dark and greasy. He smiled at her, showing rotting teeth.

"I'm sorry I frightened you," he said. "You're a kind girl. I was a respectable man once, when I had my legs. You will remember that, won't you?"

"Yes, I'll remember. I promise."

"God bless you, Miss. Get home now. A young lady like you shouldn't be out alone."

Edwina went on her way feeling – once she was far enough away and her heart was beating normally – quite proud of being so brave. Even Caroline Emerson was frightened of the legless beggar and she was hardly ever frightened of anything. Still, she mustn't stop again or she'd be away too long. She hurried to join a group of people crossing the road where the crossing sweeper worked in his long white coat, wishing she had glazed kid boots to protect from horse manure, like the elegant ladies around her, instead of her black leather ones. Nobody noticed her being alone, nobody even imagined it, each group thinking she belonged to some other group. Besides, they were all busy talking, saying boring Sunday afternoon things and nodding and bowing to each other. Edwina turned into the avenue of chestnut trees where it was quieter and there she saw the noisy motor car which Jim had admired yesterday. It was slower than a carriage and four and its hooter made a rasping ugly noise in the hope of persuading a brown dog sitting in the road to get out of the way. The brown dog, half asleep in the pleasant sunshine, lifted its head and yawned, watched curiously as the car manoeuvred round him and settled down to doze again. Edwina would have liked to go up to him and stroke his warm sleepy head but May's dire warning about fleas and bites and rabies stopped her. On her right, the usual dejected horses stood in the field. If only, Edwina thought, she had an aunt and uncle in the country like Caroline Emerson. Not just to go barefoot, if that were really true, but because there, according to Caroline, the horses came trotting towards you, whinnying with joy, to search your pockets for bits of sugar or an apple. These horses stared at Edwina without moving. Perhaps nobody had ever offered them anything. Even so, they went on staring at her because they had nothing else to look at and there was nothing fit to eat in the churned-up field, just poisonous-looking weeds blackened by city smoke. Edwina held out her hand.

"Do come," she said. "Please come and be stroked." They went on staring, their eyes dull, but then one of them, either bored or curious, came plodding towards her.

"Good boy! Come on!" Edwina was delighted – but what was she to give him? She did have some little pieces of sugar and – of course! There were a few slices of apple. It wasn't much but he looked so hungry and sad and he watched her intently as she pulled the full napkin out of the pinafore pocket under her fawn coat. She opened it carefully so as not to spill things, talking to him as she did so.

"I can't give you so very much because of the poor crippled girl but you can have— oh!" Too late, she stepped back. The poor hungry beast had snapped at the napkin and was chewing bits of sugar, raisins, apple and even the chicken patties and a corner of the napkin, neither of which he liked and which made him twist and lift his upper lip at their strangeness. All the food had gone. Edwina pulled at the trailing napkin until he released it and then the two of them stood looking at one another, neither of them sure what to do next.

"I haven't got anything else," she told him, "except a florin and you don't want that." She took the florin from her pinafore pocket now and stuffed the empty napkin in its place. The florin she slipped into her kid glove, ready to give to the girl. The horse, hoping for more treasure, stretched his neck and nuzzled at her gloved hand, licking like a cat.

"There's nothing. You can see." But there had been nothing before and out of nothing something eatable had sprung. He licked and licked, his hopes awakened by that little bit of kindness, leaving a trail of dirty green saliva and sugar stickiness on her kid gloves and her best fawn coat.

"Oh… oh dear…" She tried to distract him by patting his neck but that only dirtied her glove even more while the poor hopeful creature, wondering if her hat might be eatable, snapped at that and broke the elastic so that it fell on the dirty ground.

"Oh no!" Edwina picked it up and hurried on under the chestnut trees, afraid to look back and see the sad eyes watching her go. Faster and faster she walked until, by the time she turned off the avenue into the narrow street, she was running. She ran with her head down so that nothing else could distract her. The next thing she knew she had crashed head first into somebody and the somebody grabbed viciously at her arm, spinning her round. Someone else hit her from behind and her hair was yanked and her coat dragged at until its buttons popped off. She was too terrified to breathe, never mind scream, but she fought and struggled until at last they let her go and stood around her in a circle, laughing and sneering. They were the ragged boys who had been throwing stones the day before. What would they do to her? Would they kill her?

"Where d'you think you're going, then?"

"You don't belong round here in your fancy clothes."

"What'll you give us for not slitting your throat?"

"See this?" One of them waved a knife under her nose and the others laughed.

Edwina's legs started wobbling and she was going to be sick. Perhaps, more than anything, it was the fear of being sick right there in the street in front of all those eyes that made her move and save herself. She tore back her glove, took the florin and, letting them see what it was, threw it as far away as she could. They ran after it, shouting, and Edwina rushed on down the street and crashed in at Katy's front door.

Even as she slammed it behind her in her panic it crossed her mind that it was odd she should have been so sure, without thinking or looking, which door it was, but whatever the reason she had been right. The white-faced girl was there, standing right before her in the gloom with a cracked cup in her hands and the frightening black irons on her crooked legs. She didn't speak. Edwina heard nothing but her own loud breathing and heartbeat and she saw nothing at first except the girl. She was staring at Edwina who was red-faced and hot in her thick fawn coat with its cape trimmed with brown braid and its buttons torn off. Edwina stared back. The girl wore a patched blue frock and pinafore and no socks protected her legs from the hardness of her clogs and irons. She looked cold. The small room, its window covered by a bit of unbleached cotton tacked across it for a curtain, was very dark and the black grate was well polished but held only a very little fire. As Edwina's eyes adjusted themselves to the gloom, she realised that there was another person there, an old woman sitting in a broken and sagging armchair near the fireplace. She was busy with a lumpy-looking cloth thing in her lap and although her head was lifted from her work as though she had heard Edwina burst in, she didn't look towards the door.

"Who's that?" she asked, still without looking.

"I don't know," said the crippled girl, her eyes fixed on Edwina's.

There was such a strong smell in the room that Edwina found it hard not to be very rude and screw her nose up. She wasn't sure what it was but part of it was a dirty washing sort of smell which she recognised from Marjorie Weaks's laundry days. There were other smells here, too, though, and the strongest of these was something she had smelled before, something horrible that she had made herself forget. She knew she ought to explain who she was and apologise for bursting in like that. It was a dreadful thing to do, so dreadful that Edwina couldn't begin to excuse or explain it. And yet the girl in front of her seemed more frightened and embarrassed than herself and it was she who seemed anxious to excuse and explain.

"I didn't come to church because I was helping my grandma, please Miss."

"Who's there, Katherine? Is it the lady from the parish?"

"No grandma. I think it must be one of her daughters. D'you remember how one daughter came with her once and brought me some boots?"

"Ah. Well, let the young lady sit herself down and you go out and fill the kettle to make my tea, will you? There's a good girl."

There was only one hard chair in the small room and the little girl dragged it away from the table with difficulty. Edwina, not knowing what to do or say, sat down.

"Thank you." Really she was quite glad to sit down. After all her running and the shock of the boys' attack she was still shaking. Dragging her stiff, splinted legs, the girl took the iron kettle and went outside. In silence Edwina watched her go, then turned her attention to the old woman by the fire.

"What are you making?" she asked after a while, for she wasn't at all afraid of the old woman whose face, now she could make it out, was as kind and gentle as her voice. "You're very clever to work without a candle in this dark room. You must have very good eyes."

"No Miss. My eyes are very bad and that's why I've no use for a candle. My fingers are my eyes, these days, and Katherine helps me choose the colours. We're making a new rag rug for the hearth. The old one has a lot of burns in it now."

Edwina came closer. The old hearth rug was certainly flattened and dirty and some of the holes made in it by sparks and falling coals were quite big.

"I've never seen anyone make a rug," said Edwina, who thought you bought rugs in shops. "Is it very difficult? Where do you get all those strips of cloth? And how do you make them come out in that pattern? Is that a star in the middle?"

At home she would have been told off for making a nuisance of herself with so many questions but the old lady only smiled as her fingers felt their way along the piece of sacking and poked another coloured strip through it with a wooden clothes peg.

"Katherine did the star," she said. "She cuts the strips from old clothes and arranges them in piles of one colour. I'm doing a brown stripe now, do you see? I can't do without her, Miss, not these days. I've worked in the mill since I was five years old and I can still weave. There's never a fault in my cloth, but the days when I could manage eight looms are gone. Katherine has four of them now and helps with mine besides. If I were to send her to school of an afternoon, like I should, we wouldn't earn enough to eat. And when I used to send her, she'd get the cane for falling asleep during her lessons. I do send her to church when I can, when I've a penny to spare for the collection. You will tell your mother? You will explain to her and tell her we're sorry?"

"But I… Yes, I'll explain." How could she say who she really was? She didn't know how.

"It makes me ashamed to think as she came specially with a pair of right good cast-off boots for the child, thinking that's why I couldn't send her to church. She can't get them on, not with the irons. That's why she only wears her clogs, no offence meant. But she gives the boots a good rubbing every day. She's a grateful girl. You didn't bring her a drop of milk?"

"Milk…? No, I couldn't steal— I mean, no. I'm sorry."

"It was milk she needed. That's what they said when they put the irons on her. But with her mother dying right after she was born, what was I to do? I gave her plenty of flour and water but they say that doesn't do for them. They drink it, right enough, but they don't thrive the same, so they tell me."

Edwina was silent, trying to understand. After a while, thinking over what the old woman had said before and with the school problem never far from her mind, she asked, "Does Katy – Katherine – not want to go to school? I do and I don't think it's fair not being allowed to go."

What had she said? The poor woman looked frightened and her hands shook as she turned a brown strip over and over between them. "It's the school inspector, isn't it? He's been talking to your mother, hasn't he, Miss? Dear God, how do they expect us to manage? We have to eat. Besides, she'll soon be twelve, anyway, and if I'd given up my looms to somebody else who didn't help me – oh,

you'll not tell your mother that, though, will you?
If the Inspector comes round—"

"I won't say anything to anyone, ever. Please
don't be afraid. I never tell tales and, if you want me
to, I'll say that she does go to school. I want to go
but my parents can't send me, either." She wanted
to ask about the girl working in the mill but it
didn't seem polite. She had seen a cotton mill once
when Papa had taken her to see a new engine he
had designed. Jim had been only a baby and Papa
hadn't begun designing motor car engines yet. It
had been a terrifying experience which had made
her have nightmares for months afterwards so that
Mamma had been furious with him. He had
stopped doing things like that to her once Jim was
big enough to admire his work but the suffocating
smell of raw cotton, the deafening noise and the
gigantic gnashing looms stayed in her memory
even now. She had seen children there, carrying
enormous baskets of spools and crawling beneath
the crashing jaws of the machinery to clean out
piles of fluff, but she still couldn't believe that it was
real, that normal people thought it a normal place.
It was worse than she had ever imagined hell to be
and, besides, the people inside couldn't have been
normal because they grinned and chatted to each

other as though there were no deafening noise at all. Papa had explained to her that they could lip read, but how? And how could they breathe and how could they not cover their ears against the crashing din that hurt so desperately inside her head that she screamed to be taken out? Screams that made no sound until she got outside and collapsed, hoarse and sobbing into Papa's arms. Then the bellowing wail of a siren started up and she started screaming again, even though Papa laughed at her and said it was only to sound the end of the working day. It was the dank and oily cotton mill smell that she had recognised in this room.

"Here she comes." The old woman lifted her head, her ears evidently better than her eyes for Edwina heard nothing until the door opened and the girl brought in the big kettle and hung it over the meagre fire.

Then she looked at Edwina and asked, "D'you want my grandma to mend it for you?"

Edwina only stared, not understanding. Then she saw that the girl was looking at her hat with its trailing elastic.

"Oh! Would she mend it for me?" Without thinking she passed over the hat.

"The elastic's broken on the young lady's hat, grandma."

"What colour hat is it? Give me a needle and thread," the old woman said, feeling round the band inside and finding the broken elastic.

"It's fawn-coloured." Edwina was so used to May's mending everything she tore or broke that the work was begun before it crossed her mind that, if they were so poor, it should be paid for.

But I shall give them the florin, anyway, she thought, so that's all right.

The mending was done in a moment and the hat handed back to her. "There you are, Miss. Now you'll not mind if I have my cup of tea? Is the water boiling, love?"

"It won't be a minute, Grandma." The kettle was hissing over the bit of fire and the girl was spooning half a teaspoon of tea into a chipped enamel teapot.

"Shall I help you?" Edwina asked, wanting to be thought as clever and grown-up as this girl who went out to work and was allowed to mess with fire and boiling water. She had watched May often enough to know what had to be done. "I could butter the bread though I'm not allowed to cut it because the bread knife's dangerous but I can cut cake because the cake knife isn't so sharp and if you're having an egg, I know how long it takes to make it go hard. I hate soft-boiled eggs, don't you? And I could spoon the jam into its dish. Do you have jam on Sundays? We do and I *wish* we had it every day, don't you? I wish we could always have bread and jam for breakfast, too, instead of porridge. Don't you just *hate* porridge?"

The girl didn't answer but her white face turned red for a moment before going pale again. Edwina thought she saw tears in her eyes but the girl turned away too quickly for her to be sure.

"We just have some porridge on Sundays for our dinner. We don't have anything else." She went close to the fire to brew her grandmother's tea.

They want me to go away, Edwina thought. She didn't know how she knew but she knew. The old woman had put down her work ready for her tea and, while she waited for it, she took from the mantle shelf above her head a clay pipe into which she pushed the tiniest pinch of tobacco from a tin, lighting it with a wood spill poked into the fire. That's what the other smell was in the room: mixed up with the dirty washing smell and the cotton mill smell was the pipe tobacco smell, Papa's smell. She had never seen a woman smoking before but she had never seen people with no Sunday tea before either. She wanted to run away to the comfortable chair by the nursery fire and buttered toast and May. The only thing that stopped her was remembering this little girl as she had seen her yesterday, her small face so solemn and glowing in its whiteness at her joy in dancing only with her arms. It wasn't all this poverty and sadness which made Edwina's heart ache in her chest, but that tiny secret joy which nothing had managed to crush, not even the ugly irons on her thin legs.

"I saw you dancing," she blurted out as Katherine put the teacup in her grandmother's hands. "I saw you… yesterday and I wanted to help you."

The girl dragged towards her and stood waiting, obedient, to be offered charity.

In a sudden wave Edwina remembered it all: the flower seller, the legless beggar, the sad horse and the thieving boys. There was nothing left… Nothing…

"I wanted to… I wanted…" Her hands were plunging, groping in her pockets for something, anything, to give. Still the girl stood waiting, and when Edwina's searching hand pulled out the only thing she had left, Katherine darted forward, grabbed, thanked her and stuffed something quickly into her mouth. She chewed rapidly, her gaze fixed and intense just like the sad horse. In Edwina's hand was the bag of stale crusts for the swans.

With a cry of dismay Edwina turned and ran out of the house, forgetful of the street boys, forgetful of the pretty posy which she had dropped when they attacked her and which she now crushed under her boots as she ran away.

⟶ CHAPTER TEN ⟶

ALL SHE WANTED to remember was the way home to May and Jim and Mamma and Papa and safe Sunday tea in the quiet drawing room. She ran her fastest through the streets she had thought were exciting but now were only frightening. All the warmth had gone from the sun as it sank below St Paul's Church spire behind her. People were coming towards her as the church bell summoned them to evensong and Edwina heard the start of a hymn played on the organ. How late could it be?

What had she done? The air smelled of coolness, of evening, of bedtime. Fear of the streets was pushed into the background as fear of a spanking from May grew inside her. And if May had given up looking and gone home and told Mamma? A little whine of fear escaped her as she tried to run even faster, her heart thudding as loudly as her boots, her lungs hurting fit to burst. How could she have done something so stupid? How could she have imagined she would get away with it? She knew that she should have been content to put Mamma's florin into the collection box but how could it be fair that it was naughty to try and help? It wasn't fair. It wasn't! Edwina thudded along the avenue, sending up dead leaves behind her, giving a tiny sob every so often. Her hair was tumbling loose from its ribbon. She felt like crying her heart out but she had no breath for it. The avenue looked cold and sad. The day was fading and those who hadn't gone to church were at home by now having tea. Before she reached the end of the avenue Edwina stopped, remembering the sad hopeful gaze of the horse.

"No…" She couldn't stand any more sadness, any more hopeful eyes waiting for help she couldn't give. "I have to find another way home, I *have* to. Just for a second she hesitated, trying to decide whether to make for home or the park. Home, she decided, partly because she knew from the empty streets that it was too late to try the park but mostly because she just wanted to go home. Even a spanking was better than being out in the wicked world alone. So she ran on down a street she didn't know which seemed like the right direction for home. It was the worst way she could have chosen but she had no way of knowing that. She was running in the shadow of a huge black stone building on her left. Its tall windows were too high above her head for her to see in, but ahead of her was an entrance with steps up to it and she saw two nurses in long blue cloaks come down and walk across the road. It was the hospital and she was safe. She knew the road behind the hospital was a shortcut that would take her to Millbridge Road and home because May had told her so. They never used it because May said you'd catch some dreadful disease just by breathing the air coming through the doors of the place. She said the people in there were dying of putrid fevers and were covered in running sores. Edwina slowed down and dried her eyes on her coat sleeve, wondering if it might be safer to cross and walk on the other side. Then she saw a lot of people, many of them children, going towards the hospital and climbing the steps. They weren't ill because some of them were running. Edwina went nearer and then waited to see what was happening. As she came close, the hospital doors opened and two porters came out carrying a gigantic tin bowl which they dumped on the broad top step. Edwina only just got a glimpse of the great mound of waste food left by the sick and dying: porridge and potatoes, stewed meat and rice pudding, sodden bread, boiled cabbage and slithering custard, before the crowd dived forward, reaching with greedy hands. May's warnings of putrid fevers and running sores rose up in Edwina's mind and mixed themselves into the slimy cold mess and she got hold of the nearest little girl.

"Don't! Oh don't!" But the child wrenched her arm free and spat at Edwina, kicking out in defence of her treasure with a filthy bare leg covered in scabs. Custard and cabbage slid down her chin as she crammed the precious food into her mouth, her hair stiff and matted, her eyes as fierce as a tiger's.

Edwina turned and ran, her hand clapped to her mouth as she retched and retched, but her empty stomach brought up nothing except saliva.

She didn't cry now, didn't scream. She was inside a nightmare. She couldn't feel her running legs or hear her gasping breath. She couldn't tell where she was running to or take notice of the many people she banged against until one of them stopped her and held both her shoulders with his huge, meaty hands.

"Now then, Miss. I think they're waiting for you at home. You just come along with me."

It was May's policeman.

Edwina sat on her bed watching in silence as the sun set behind the chimneys opposite beyond the barred window. The worst had happened. May had rushed home with Jim, both of them in tears, and told Mamma. The full story of her planned adventure had been got out of Jim, and May had already packed her bags and left by the time Edwina was brought home. Mamma's face… She couldn't bear to think of it. And how could she bear life without May's cheerfulness, May's understanding and her stories and her comforting arms. Edwina hated herself for what she'd done but she hated Jim more. If he hadn't gone and told, it would have been possible to pretend that she had only wandered a bit too far away and got lost.

Anybody can get lost. Perhaps May would have been sent away just the same for not keeping an eye on her but at least Mamma wouldn't have looked at her like that.

"You look so… wild. Go upstairs, please. Go at once." And she had turned away, unable to bear looking at her wild and wicked daughter. There had been tears in her eyes. Edwina had seen herself in the hall mirror as she left the drawing room. Her hair was tumbled and knotted, her ribbon gone. Her coat was torn open, her hat missing, her gloves and coat sleeves smeared with dirt. Her face was red and streaked with dirty tears and her eyes glittered with fright. It was true that she looked wild, like a frightened animal. Now she sat on the bed, still in her coat, too miserable to move. All May's terrible warnings returned to torment her. All the things she had despised, from porridge to respectable petticoats, had taken on a different meaning, a terrifying meaning, connected with leg irons, cotton mills and the girl with matted hair and infected slops running down her chin. That's what Edwina had thought about her, that she looked like a wild animal as she spat and kicked and glared at Edwina with glittering, desperate eyes to defend her food.

"You look so... wild."

"Oh Mamma! Don't hate me!" This wasn't what she had wanted. It wasn't what she had imagined. She had seen herself graciously helping the poor dancing girl and she still didn't understand how or why it had all gone so wrong. She stood up and looked out of the window with a feeling of panic rising inside her. Nothing she wanted to do had worked: she hadn't helped that poor girl, she hadn't grown up into a beautiful woman dressed in lace and scented with violets like Mamma, she hadn't become a famous musician. She stood there with her palms and forehead pressed against the cold glass and let herself cry. The light was fading and the sadness of the dying day overwhelmed her.

"And now it's too late. It's all too late and I can't put it right. I've disappointed everybody and helped nobody and harmed May and now I'll never play my flute again. It's all over." As if to confirm what she said, the day ended and the red sun slipped down behind the black roof of the house across the way. One last ray blinded her for a moment. She looked down to protect her sore, weeping eyes and saw a girl standing there looking up, a girl with tumbled hair like her own but wearing funny clothes. For some reason, the sight of her made

Edwina stop crying, as though there were one last thing to hope for. She felt for a handkerchief in her pinafore pocket and dried her eyes. When she looked down again the street was empty. Even so, her feeling of panic was gone and she set about getting herself ready for bed as best she could without May. She would never be able to untangle her hair alone so she got into her nightdress and just left it as it was. She knew there was no point any more in worrying about it but she didn't stop to ask herself why. It was cool and quiet in bed in the half dark. She thought of Jim, down in the gas-lit drawing room, stuffed full of bread and jam and cake, looking at photographs and drawings of the Ghost with Papa. Usually, at this time Edwina would have been there playing her flute after Sunday tea. Mamma would smile and clap and Papa would ask for his favourite piece of which he could never remember the name. Her feeling of panic was quite gone now and she only felt quiet and sad. After a while she reached for her music box and wound it up. The little dancer twirled to the music and Edwina watched quietly, thinking of Katherine whom she had called Katy, but without crying now. As the music wound down, she heard Marjorie Weaks come clattering up the attic stairs bringing

Jim to bed. He had already been scrubbed to shining pinkness for drawing-room tea and Marjorie Weaks certainly had no time to waste on stories or last drinks of water and said so.

"And in the morning you dress yourselves. I've my slops to do and the fires and breakfast to serve. It's not my place to be waiting on you. Some people might think on a bit before firing servants and expecting others to do their work."

"I can easily dress myself," said Jim, "and I don't want you to dress me. I don't want you to come anywhere near me. I hate you and I want May."

"Well, it's a shame for you is all I can say because she's never coming back and serves you both right. Now get to bed and no messing."

"Wait!" Jim had been shouting but now his voice became a frightened whine. "I've no night-light. You have to light one for me, you have to."

"Light it yourself," snapped Marjorie Weaks as she went out the door.

"I can't because it's finished! You have to bring me up a new one from Mamma's cupboard and you have to light it because I'm not allowed!"

"If you think I'm climbing these stairs again you've got another think coming. It's not my place and that's that."

"Marjorie Weaks! Marjorie Weaks, come back! Come back at once or I'll tell Mamma!"

But Marjorie Weaks had gone. It was quite dark in the room now and Edwina felt herself falling asleep but after a short silence she heard Jim's tiny voice.

"I have to have my night-light. Will you go down and tell Mamma, Edwina?"

"Go yourself. I'm nearly asleep."

There was silence again but soon she heard him crying in the dark. She felt too tired to move and, anyway, it was his fault that May had got the sack just as much as hers. She felt guilty enough to say, "It's only for one night. You can ask Mamma for one in the morning."

"You ask her now, *please*, Edwina."

"You know I can't. I've been sent to bed. Mamma hates me. I can't go down." She tried to sink into sleep again but she could hear him crying, trying to hide under the bedclothes from all the house's ghosts and monsters who, once they heard he had no nightlight, would be creeping towards the dark nursery. After some time he stopped crying and Edwina heard him get out of bed and go next door, padding across the day nursery linoleum in his bare feet. She opened her eyes. She couldn't see anything other than the faint pale patch of Jim's turned-back sheets. Then she heard the door from the day nursery to the corridor open and close.

"Jim…?"

He would never dare go downstairs by himself. He couldn't. He wouldn't even brave the creaking stair alone, never mind the coffin cupboard and the ragged old woman in the clock and the red-hot ghosts on the landing.

"Jim?" He couldn't possibly. Not alone in the dark, not without a candle…

"Oh, no… Jim, no!" Shocked awake, Edwina jumped out of bed and ran across the cold linoleum. Stubbing her toe on the end of his bed she scrabbled at his bedside chest. His night-light matches were gone. As she ran into the day nursery she heard him strike one outside the door.

"*Jim!*" she screamed but she was too late and her sudden scream must have terrified the already nervous child. She heard the brass lamp hit the floor and its glass globe shatter. Under the door a burning trickle snaked towards her bare feet.

"I didn't, I didn't! Don't tell, Edwina, oh don't tell, don't, don't… oh…"

She heard the breathless panic in his voice and realised that he was still standing out there paralysed with fear instead of running away. He ought to run away but the world seemed to be turning so slowly that her own limbs were like lead, they were so heavy.

Edwina made a huge effort and took a step backwards. The little river of fire followed her, eating up the linoleum in its path and starting to lick at the edge of the rug. The paint on the door bubbled up in hissing blisters and burst into flames. It was not fear but heat that drove Edwina back to the night nursery where she shut the door and leaned her back against it as though that would keep her safe. She stood like that for some time, her eyes wide open but seeing nothing. Beyond the door the fire was roaring now, fed by old wooden furniture, paint and cloth. She could still hear Jim repeating over and over, "I can't go by myself, I can't! Somebody help me." He wasn't shouting any more, just saying it without any expression in his voice, a voice that seemed to reach Edwina from far away. Then smoke came in, in spite of the closed door. It must have crept in underneath and around the edges though Edwina couldn't see well enough to be sure. It surrounded her, choking her with its terrible stink of burnt wool and melted paint and the door became too hot to lean against. Edwina rushed to the window and wrestled with the stiff catch. She managed to get it open and cough smoke out into the night air but more and more of it billowed round her, sucked towards the window by the cold draught.

"I can't go by myself. Somebody help me." Was that still Jim's voice? She held the bars as she coughed and coughed and the heat behind her grew fiercer. You'd think the girl down in the street would get help, make someone call the fire brigade. Of course, it was useless. The whole day nursery was burning and she knew by the heat and brightness behind her that this room was alight, too. They couldn't get in the windows because of the bars which were warm now. Her hot hands sweated and slid as she clung to them.

"I can't help you. I can't…" That wasn't Jim, it was the girl down in the street. Edwina couldn't see her now that everything was red but she wanted to tell her that, anyway, it was too late, just as she'd known it would be. She couldn't breathe even enough to cough now and she was too dizzy to feel the searing pain that ripped up her back and tore at her hair and frizzled it. She knew it was there but the only feeling was a last wave of deep sadness for the small, sweet things of life that she didn't want to leave: her mother's scented hands, the smell of an autumn evening in the street with the little dancing girls, the feel of the furry blue lining of her flute case, the smells of morning in the pantry, the sad eyes of a horse, Jim in the mail cart shouting "Play with me Edwina, Play with me…".

Too late. The red world darkened and went black.

~ CHAPTER ELEVEN ~

"I'M BURNING… OH Mamma, help me, I'm burning."

"I know, sweetheart. Just lie still, you'll be all right."

But it wasn't all right so why did she say that? Even so, something icy touched her forehead and cooled it. That was good but it didn't last. The fire licked at it and blazed up again.

"Mamma!" In her distress and torment she knew she must find some water and that, despite the voices which spoke to her every now and then, nobody could reach her. Nobody could help. She must keep going and find water. In the park there was a lake, a big cool grey lake. That would be the best place to go if only she could find it and if only she weren't so tired and sick and her legs didn't ache so.

"Is it the Boers?" the blind beggar asked.

"No, it's rickets. Please will you tell me the way to the park? You're so kind and I was respectable once when May was here."

He talked to her for a long time and he was very kind so that she felt soothed and quiet but she couldn't hear his words. She couldn't even hear her own words though she was answering him. She could only feel his kindness and sense the beams of friendliness shining from his face and she couldn't understand how anyone could ever have been afraid of him.

"I have to go now because I'm very tired and my legs hurt."

Did she say that or did he? It didn't really matter because she had to go and find the park and the cool water. If only she wasn't too late!

It was such a long, long way and the pavement dipped and swayed under her feet as if she were on a raft in a rough sea.

"Hold my hand. Oh please, please don't let me fall!"

"I'm holding your hand. Lie still."

"No! I have to keep going. Hold my hand. Don't let me go. You mustn't let me go! Hold it tighter. Tighter!"

The little girl walking beside her squeezed her hand until it hurt and she felt safer. They were moving forward now, even though her legs didn't seem to be walking. She looked at the little girl. How changed she was. She was dressed in pretty clothes and well-polished boots. Her face, once dirty and dribbling waste food, was clean and smiling. Her hair was no longer filthy and matted but dressed in long shining sausage curls.

"May did them for me. She combed them round her finger and I'm going to dancing class. You can't go any more because you're dead."

"I know." She was so weighed down by sadness, so lonely. "Please hold my hand and don't leave me. If we can only reach the lake in time it will be all right. This is only a nightmare, you know, but I do feel very ill."

They walked a long way in silence and then she said, as loudly as she could, "I can't breathe."

Something touched her face and a voice said,

"This will help you. Breathe quietly."

"It's not enough. I still can't breathe. It's getting hotter…"

They hadn't reached the park. This big black building was the cotton mill and she recognised it at once from the high windows and the nurses coming down the steps.

"I don't want to go in there!"

"You have to. They're going to put irons on your legs."

"No!" But she couldn't stop them. They had got hold of her and were tying something around her tightly. The steep coal shute gaped in front of her and they were going to push her down there into the hot smelly darkness. She felt herself being lifted.

"No! My legs! No, please!" She clung to the hand that held hers as she was bumped about and the noise grew louder. "Don't let me go!"

"I won't. It's all right. I'm coming with you."

But it wasn't all right. She was sliding faster and faster down the shute and there was nothing she could do to stop herself. She screamed and screamed and screamed but the roaring heat and the crashing machines that would mangle her legs drowned her cries.

The big siren started to wail.

"How are you feeling now?"

She wanted to say she was thirsty but she was too exhausted to speak. She thought she would try opening her eyes and at once she saw Katy, dressed in white, standing a long way away beckoning to her.

"Katy! You're wearing your Easter dress! It's not too late, then?"

"No. Come with me."

She got up and they walked together out into the park across the fresh sweet grass to the lake.

"Did you bring me some bread?" Katy asked as she slipped into the water and curved her pure white neck to look at her reflection.

"Yes. It's in my pocket." Everything was all right, after all. She took out the bag of bread and began tossing the pieces into the glassy grey water. The swan took them, splashing softly with its yellow bill and sailing gracefully round and round to the music. It was so peaceful there with the grassy smells and the gentle lapping of the water. With a happy sigh, she stepped out of her hot boots and stockings and felt the tickle of grass beneath her feet as she went towards the water and sank gratefully into its coolness.

"She'll be all right, now," said a voice.

"Yes," Carrie answered, "I'm all right now." Then she slept.

The next time Carrie opened her eyes, it was dark and she could see nothing. After a while she made out a few shapes in the room but there was nothing that she recognised. There was what seemed to be a window with something pale hanging in front of it that could be a Venetian blind. This wasn't her bedroom. These weren't her bedclothes, either. She felt the stiff cotton coverlet with her hand. She had no idea where she was and, worse still, her nightdress and the sheet beneath her felt soaking wet. Surely she couldn't have wet the bed? She was far too old for that to happen. She tried to remember exactly how old she was but she couldn't and, anyway, the effort hurt her head. Still, the bed was certainly wet and it was somebody else's bed, not hers. Where could she be? What was the last thing she remembered doing? Katy! She had been with Katy and they'd gone to the park. She'd been at Katy's house, too, that was it… she must have stayed the night. So this was Katy's bedroom and that pale shape on her right must be Katy's lumpy old bed and she was there asleep.

What on earth was she to do about the wet sheets? She tried to get out of bed to see if she could change them but the minute she sat up everything began spinning and buzzing in her head and she found she was fainting and had to lie back again. She would run away, then, run home. But if she couldn't even sit up how could she find the strength to run home in the cold night? It was very cold, even in here, and Carrie shivered as she wondered why Katy's house was so very poor and cold and sad now. It didn't used to be as bad as this. And now Katy's gran would find the wet sheets in the morning. There was nothing to be done about it. She was too cold and weak and tired to move. She began to cry.

"What's the matter?" whispered a voice from the next bed. It wasn't Katy's voice so whose house could this be?

"I don't know where I am," sobbed Carrie, "and I've wet the sheets and I feel too ill to get up and change them and I'm freezing cold."

"It's all right," the girl said, "I'll ring the bell and they'll change the sheets for you."

'Oh, please don't tell anybody," begged Carrie, "I don't want anyone to know what I've done and I don't even know whose house this is. I can't remember where I am."

"You're in hospital," the girl said and Carrie saw her faint shape sitting up in the dark. "This isn't anybody's house, it's a hospital so it doesn't matter a bit if your sheets need changing. I'll ring the bell and the nurse will come and do it. They've changed them twice already tonight because you've got a fever and you sweat."

"Have I? Are you sure that's what it is?"

"Positive. One of the nurses told me and your mum said you've got pneumonia."

"My mum?"

"Yes. She's here all the time. I expect she's gone to get a cup of tea."

"A cup of tea…"

"You're funny. Why do you repeat everything I say like that?"

Carrie didn't answer. Her mum… her mum was here, somewhere nearby. A cup of tea… What lovely things to think about, her mum… a cup of tea… and this was a hospital so it didn't matter about the sheets. Carrie smiled in the darkness and closed her eyes. Everything was all right. Her mum… a cup of tea…

The next time she woke up she was warm and comfortable and remembered this was a hospital. She moved her legs carefully, then kicked, then squeezed her ankles together. There were no irons.

Just to be sure, she felt under the bedclothes and checked. They hadn't done it yet. In the morning she could tell them there was no need. With a happy sigh, she fell asleep, smiling.

"Are you with us this morning? Will I bring you a bit of breakfast?"

Carrie recognised the voice and felt sunlight on her eyelids. A bird was chirrupping. She opened her eyes.

"May! You're here!"

"And where else would I be? Wasn't I here every morning to let your mammy go home to Jim for an hour? And this is the first time you've taken the trouble to speak to me."

"Oh, May, I'm so glad to see you!" Carrie held out her arms and May hugged her, whispering, "Oh, you did give us a fright. Your mammy's been out of her mind and your daddy's come home from Hong Kong in such a panic. Let me look at you. Your face is so thin but your head's cool now. Do you feel all right?"

"I feel great. May, that girl in the next bed said I had pneumonia. Did I?"

"Indeed you did and no wonder, getting soaked to the skin and catching a cold and then going up there in that freezing attic. What made you do it we'll never know. You'd a fever that would set the place on fire. Delirious, too."

"Was I? May, that's as good as the people in your stories, like your aunty Mary. She was delirious. Will you tell people about me, May?"

"I've told them at home already. My mammy's sent you a loaf of her best soda bread and a little bunch of shamrock for luck."

"Shamrock? I've never seen shamrock. Can you really post it?"

"Can you post it? We post tons of it all over the world for St Patrick's Day. Can you post it, indeed! Look there." In a pool of sunshine on the locker stood a little water glass crowded with tiny clover-like leaves that spilled over its edges in a cascade of emerald green. Next to it a chunky round loaf peeped from its paper bag.

"Now, will I bring you some breakfast?"

"Can I have some breakfast? I am hungry and I'm very thirsty…" That lovely fresh green, the sunshine, the chirping bird, the bread in a paper bag reminded her of something…

"I'll cut you a slice and bring you soda bread and butter and a nice cup of tea. Would you like that?"

"I'd love it… May, they won't mind if I don't have porridge? If I'm supposed to I will."

"Porridge, is it? And what in the world made you think of porridge? You never have it at home and you've not been given it here, that's for sure, for you've eaten nothing at all, so why porridge?"

"I don't know. I just thought… I don't know…"

"I'll get your breakfast. That way, when your mammy gets back she'll find you sitting up and eating and won't she be surprised." May took the loaf in its bag, winked at Carrie and went out.

Carrie looked again at the shamrock, then at the girl in the next bed who had eaten her breakfast and gone back to sleep. Her tray was on a little table swung out from her locker and there was an egg cup with broken shells and a piece of white bread and butter on a plate. For some reason Carrie wanted to take that slice of bread. Her hand reached out but she pulled it back quickly, remembering May's warning.

"You'd catch some dreadful disease just by breathing the air coming through the doors of the place."

Had May really said that? Surely, she couldn't have. This was the clean new hospital not far from home. A faint, unpleasant memory about leftover food and hospitals faded away and was replaced by a memory of bread and butter on a pretty flowered plate in a warm room scented with violets. Carrie closed her eyes and lay still, not forcing herself to try and sort these muddled memories out. They could come and go as they pleased. It didn't matter. What mattered was the warm sun on her face, the chirping bird, Mum and Dad coming soon, May and breakfast. She felt very happy. May's mum's soda bread was so good that Carrie could have eaten the whole loaf.

"My goodness," May said, amazed. "I never saw you with such an appetite, and you supposed to be ill."

"I'm not ill, May, not any more. And it's so good. May, are my legs all right? I mean, if you get delirious does it do something to your legs?"

"Of course not! Oh, you'll feel a bit wobbly when you first get up after your fever but that's nothing at all. What made you think that, now, is a mystery. Sure, you nearly had the ambulance men killed when we brought you here. They thought they'd never get you fastened on the stretcher with you kicking and shouting the way you did. Do you remember that?"

"I think I do, a bit. I didn't know what they were doing to me and I was frightened of the noise, especially the siren."

"Not to mention the terrible business it was to get you into the ambulance when you wouldn't let go of your mammy's hand for so much as a second and no room for the stretcher and her to be got in at once."

"I can't remember that," Carrie said, "but I bet Jim'll be jealous because I'll be one of your best stories, May! You could tell me a story now. Will you?"

"Which story do you want? The Fairy Ring? Or will it be Michael-Joe and Sweeny's Donkey?"

"Both of them, any of them. I just want to listen to you. Go on, May."

"Well, now…"

And May went on. Carrie listened with her eyes closed and as the story went gently along, every word of it the same as always, she had time to think how good it was to hear May's voice and know that there were hundreds more stories in the world for her to hear and time to hear them, and good things to eat, and little Jim's freckles and the brace on his teeth, and Katy dancing and sunshine and the seaside and thunderstorms and umbrellas. And then she remembered that there was music. There was her flute and a world full of beautiful music which so many people had been so kind as to compose for her to play. There would be time to learn when, for some reason, she had thought there wasn't and she could be a musician when she grew up, though she thought she remembered someone saying she couldn't. It was all right. It wasn't too late. Carrie was so happy that when her mum and dad arrived they found her fast asleep and still smiling.

~ CHAPTER TWELVE ~

WHEN CARRIE CAME home from hospital everyone said that though she was thinner, she was prettier. The truth was that she was happier, happier than she could ever remember being in her life, though she couldn't explain why. On her first day home she went around the house, looking at things, feeling them, smelling them, and smiling. Not special things, just everyday things like a cake of perfumed soap, the clothes in her wardrobe, the books on the shelves, the food in the fridge, the dust on a sunbeam coming through the window.

And everybody agreed that, on the night they all sat down to talk things over and Mum was worrying and James grumbling, it was Carrie who solved everybody's problems in one go when she said to her Dad: "Well, who says we have to buy another house? Let's stay here, then you don't need to keep going to Hong Kong to earn more money. You can stay here and earn less. Then we'll all be together and we can do up this house and make it so that Gran can get about in it. Nobody will be lonely and James won't be frightened."

Her Mum and Dad stared at her, started to object and then were silent. She was right.

Carrie left them making plans, happy and excited, especially James who was already being warned in advance of the punishment he would get for playing at riding up and down the kitchen stairs on Gran's chair lift. She went quietly upstairs to the attic and stood there at the window for a long time watching, as though she were waiting for someone. Carrie had a few plans of her own.

James said that Carrie was a lot nicer after she was ill. She was a lot nicer to him, anyway, never saying he was stupid and taking him up to the attic to give him those fantastic toys and helping to mend and repaint the old rocking horse.

"*We could paint him black, Carrie, like Black Beauty, then it wouldn't matter so much when he got dirty.*"

"*No we can't. He's dappled grey and he fought with the Scots Greys at Waterloo.*"

"*How do you know?*"

"*I just know… I can't remember who told me— Oh, I expect it was in Grandad Grey's diary. It was his horse, you know.*"

Grandad Grey's diary became the explanation for a great many things which Carrie remembered and couldn't account for. She wasn't sure where those small memories came from, only that they dissolved like mist in sunshine when she tried to grasp them. After a while she got used to it and didn't worry, contenting herself with listening to whatever the memory told her without trying to make sense of it all. She learned to find great pleasure in those strange dreamy moments and let them last as long as they would. She got a reputation for being absent-minded, of course.

"*Carrie, are we going to the supermarket or are you going to sit there staring at your trainers for the rest of the afternoon? Carrie!*"

"I'm coming. Sorry. They're great these trainers, so white and soft and comfy. I got them just before I was ill, do you remember?"

"Did you? Where's that list — and remind me to put petrol in or your Dad'll shoot me... Oh, do get a move on..."

"I'm coming. Just let me tie this lace. It's a good job I don't still wear those boots with buttons all the way up."

"What boots...? I wonder if I've time to get to the bank..."

"I must have worn them when I was small and it used to take ages to button them up with a hook. May had to do it for me."

"You must have dreamt it. May's been here two years at the most. Right. Let's go."

May... Part of Carrie's plan was that May should stay and help Mum with Gran. What talks they had, what stories she told them through the winter up there in the attic. They had painted the two rooms in cheerful colours and put in heating. That was Carrie's plan, too. James had the night nursery and there he kept the precious old toy box and the smartened-up rocking horse and, of course, his secrets box. Carrie had the day nursery with the big table to do her homework on and the old cupboard, newly painted and with its doors removed, as shelves for her books and music. If ever she felt bad tempered or disappointed about something she would climb up there and, the minute she entered the low-ceilinged room, whether the sun was beaming in or the rain pattering at the barred window, that special feeling came back to her, a feeling that she was very lucky and very happy because it was good to be alive, good to be herself. And so she would feel quiet again and take up her flute to play for hours. Miss Swallow, who could hardly keep up with Carrie's progress in her flute lessons, was certainly among the people who thought Carrie was a lot nicer than she used to be. All winter long, the attic was bright and warm and filled with the cheerful noise of James's games and Carrie's music. It was a shame, Carrie said, that Gran couldn't come up and see it all and that Grandad Grey couldn't know about it when it was just what he'd always wanted.

"But he does know, sweetheart."

"Does he? How could he know, Gran?"

"He always knew. He chose your name, didn't he? And he gave you Edwina's flute. He knew. He left his diary in the toy box, too, didn't he? I'm so happy that you found it. I often read a bit of it at night when I'm

missing him, though I must say I wish my eyes were as good as yours. I've never managed to decipher any of those wonderful stories about Edwina that you tell me.

"I can't any more either. I can't find them now, but they must be there because I remember them... Aren't you glad, though, Gran, that you stayed here when he wanted it, even though you didn't understand?"

"I loved him, Carrie. I'd have done anything for him. Yes, I am glad. He was a good man."

Carrie didn't think of Grandad Grey as a good man. She had no memory of him as a man at all. When she read again in the diary of how he had nightmares and said he couldn't go by himself and tried to cover his head, she didn't see a weary soldier asleep in a muddy trench, she saw a little boy like James, frightened of the ghosts on the stairs and of something even more terrible, something red and hot... Poor Grandad Grey, poor little boy, blaming himself all his life for his sister's death and then his mother's, too. It was because of him that Carrie was so nice to James now – at least, most of the time. For instance, that creaking stair had never been fixed and he hated it, so she showed him how to sit down on the stair above, drop his feet to the one below it and then stand up.

"Besides, you can switch the light on so there's nothing to be frightened of. When I first came up here it was pitch dark!"

Katy came most days after school to do her homework with Carrie or read while she played her flute. They spent all their free time together, just like when they were smaller, and Carrie often went with her to dancing, to sit on the stairs and watch her. It gave her such a strange feeling to watch Katy dancing. Once she tried to explain it to her but couldn't. It seemed to be something to do with Katy's legs, so strong, thin as they were, and so graceful... But what was odd about that?

"I think it's something to do with my music box but I can't remember what..."

The music box remained Carrie's most precious possession. Gran had it mended for her and she intended to keep it for always. She often wound it up at bedtime and sat watching the little ballerina go round, trying to remember what it was about Katy... The memory awoke, just for a few seconds, when they gave a concert at school at the end of the Easter term. With a lot of pushing and pulling because their car was small, they managed to get Gran there, her first trip beyond the garden with her walking stick. It might have been because Gran was going to be there, though Carrie wasn't sure, that when they printed the programme she surprised her teachers by not insisting on calling herself just Carrie Grey, the way she used to. What she wanted to see written there, and what Gran then saw written there that night, was:

Solo flute ~ *Edwina Caroline Grey*

And as she began to play, wearing a new summer dress and her silver locket, she saw – in a brief flash – not the rows of parents sitting below her but a cobbled street, lit by the setting sun from behind a church spire, and little girls solemnly dancing with their pinafores held out. All except one who danced only with her arms but whose face shone with pleasure in the music. The memory faded but it left no sadness because the music went on, and Edwina Caroline went with it, not reading the notes now, not counting bars, not remembering Miss Swallow's instructions, just playing.

It was like flying.

In the summer, for her birthday, Gran gave her one of the silver photograph frames from her room for her photograph of Edwina. She kept it on the chest by her bed, next to her music box so that when the strange memories came she could talk about them to Edwina. She liked to talk about them and no one else could understand her.

One Sunday evening, that summer, she stood playing her flute near the open window. Swallows swooped and called in the rosy sky above the chimneys and the air was still sweet and warm after the long hot day. James was playing out in the back garden and Carrie heard, beyond the notes of her flute, Mum's voice shouting to him that it was bedtime. But James's voice didn't answer her and Carrie heard instead: "Play with me, Edwina! Play with me!"

She put down her flute and looked out of the window. The street was empty but she waited quietly, watching and listening, as the sun went down.

It was only a glimpse. She was walking away down the street in her fawn coat and hat and high black boots.

"Are you my twilight ghost?" Carrie asked softly as the figure moved away and began to fade, "or am I yours? Oh, don't go yet…"

She did go. She was never there for more than a few seconds. But Carrie was almost sure that, just as she reached the corner at the end of the street, she turned to look up at the attic window and that before she faded, together with the last ray of sun, she smiled.

In the dusky turquoise sky, the first star shone out.